THE MAN FROM GER

Butch Deely had been visiting his pregnant wife in hospital, and there he met Alfred Jones, who appeared to be gentle and inoffensive. But, later, Butch was to wonder about the mild-mannered man who advocated making the world a better place before bringing any more children into it. But why quarrel with a harmless crank? Then odd things began to happen in Willow Road, and it seemed as though Deely had to cope, single-handed, with a menace that could eventually descend on the entire world.

PAUL MULLER

THE MAN FROM GER

Complete and Unabridged

LINFORD
Leicester

First published in Great Britain in 1974 by
Robert Hale Limited
London

First Linford Edition
published 2003
by arrangement with
Robert Hale Limited
London

British Library CIP Data

Muller, Paul, *1924 –*
    The man from Ger.—Large print ed.—
    Linford mystery library
    1. Detective and mystery stories
    2. Large type books
    I. Title
    823.9'14 [F]

    ISBN 0–7089–4854–5

Published by
F. A. Thorpe (Publishing)
Anstey, Leicestershire

Set by Words & Graphics Ltd.
Anstey, Leicestershire
Printed and bound in Great Britain by
T. J. International Ltd., Padstow, Cornwall

This book is printed on acid-free paper

1

Butch Deely had a lot on his mind as he left the maternity wing of County Hospital and crossed the blacktop forecourt to reach his car. Mona hadn't looked too good tonight, he imagined, although she had laughed at his concern and said she was fine. The baby — their first — was almost two weeks overdue and he thought that was bad. Since the moment when he learned that his wife was pregnant Butch had been smitten with some kind of phobia. He had begun to worry about the slightest thing which he fancied might be injurious to Mona's health.

'You'll have to cut down on the smokes,' he had advised her. 'You know what they say about expectant mothers who smoke too much. Look, we'll do it together, shall we? You promise to cut out the smokes and I'll promise to do the same. We'll put the money we save into the baby's piggy-bank. By the time he's ready for school he'll have a load.'

Mona had managed to curtail the number of cigarettes she smoked daily, and the day came when she announced that she had ceased smoking altogether. Butch gave up smoking in the house and made a point of hiding his cigarettes in the automobile, smoking only when he was well clear of the house and Mona. But he did cut down on the number he bought daily and he dropped the money he saved into a money-box at the end of the week.

Then, if Mona had a sniffle, he was worrying about that. Well, a nose sniffle was the first sign of a head cold, and a head cold could travel to the chest if you weren't careful about it. He warned her about knocking herself, about lifting anything weighing heavier than a pound or so.

Of course his phobia started to tell on Mona's nerves.

'Look, darling, you'll have to stop worrying about me. You're treating me as though I were a china doll that's liable to break if you breathe more than twice on it. Forget it, will you. I come from tough peasant stock. I'm as sturdy as a jackboot. My mother had six kids and she never stopped working for longer than the time it took her to have them.'

Butch winced, but thereafter he tried to keep his worry from showing. It was no use telling himself not to worry and that everything would turn out fine. For a man who had never worried much in his life he had a huge backlog to get through.

The doctors had told him there was nothing to be alarmed about.

'Your wife is a strong, healthy woman, Mr Deely. There is nothing extraordinary about the delay in giving birth.'

'I still can't help it, Doc. I thought you usually brought a woman on.'

'Oh, we can do that, Mr Deely. But we don't think it's necessary in your wife's case. The baby will come anytime now. There might be a phone call when you arrive home.'

That was three days ago and so far the phone hadn't rung as Butch walked through the front doorway.

'I wish it would come, Butch,' Mona kept saying with a wan smile curving her lips and making sharp dimples in her full cheeks. 'I just know it's going to be a boy, darling. Little Butch. Can you see him, honey? Right now I can see him. He's going to be tall like you, and broad in the shoulders. Strong, Butch. Remember that time you and Randy got drunk? Randy said something you didn't go along with and you lifted him off the ground with your one hand.'

'Forget it. I wouldn't hurt Randy. I wouldn't hurt your brother for a million. He's not a bad guy at times. When he's sleeping, you know?'

They had laughed. Mona had taken his hairy, spatulate fingers in her own and caressed them the way she did sometimes. She kept looking into his eyes while she did so, adoring him and telling herself how lucky she was to have married Butch Deely. Butch might be nothing more than a truck driver, but she didn't mind that in the least. He got lots of overtime and earned a fair salary. Enough to have enabled them to buy their small bungalow

4

on Willow Road in Caldwell. Enough to enable them to run a second-hand car and keep a modest credit balance in their bank account.

Mona could have married Willis Vane who was teaching at the local high school now. But Willis Vane, although a nice enough fellow and an extremely bright and intelligent person, did not figure in the same league as Butch.

'He'll have your fair curly hair and your big nose. You really do have a big nose, Butch. But it's quite nice, actually. A big nose gives a man character, don't you think?'

'Sure, it does. I've got a big nose. I've got character. You hurry up and have that kid, sweetie. One thing we won't call him is Butch. Do you know what my first name is? Delmer. I wouldn't call a dog Delmer. I would call a dog Butch, though. It's a dog's name, really. We won't call our kid Butch or Delmer.'

'What shall we call him, darling?' She lifted his fingers to her mouth, kissed them with her soft lips. 'Clyde, like we said we might? Clyde like my dad? You and Dad got along, Butch.'

'We got along fine. I admired your old man, honey. Clyde Killen was a smart old gopher with plenty of brains. Given the right opportunity in his youth your dad would have gone places. Yes, we'll call the kid Clyde.'

'It might be a girl, darling,' Mona reminded him. 'She might be a girl,' she amended, smiling. 'How about that?'

'How about that? I've got nothing against girls. I married one, didn't I? Look, they're getting ready for supper, Mona. I'd better buzz off. See you tomorrow.'

'Be careful, darling. And don't worry.'

Butch kissed her on the lips and left.

It was raining and the lights down below in the town some five miles away shimmered like unsteady candle flames through the drifting veils. There were more visitors than usual at the hospital tonight, it seemed to Butch; at least there were more cars on the parking area than there normally where.

Someone had driven a Ford right up to the front of his Olds, so that he would

6

have to wait for the owner of the Ford to show up or put in a lot of manœuvring in order to reverse between two other cars at the rear of the Olds.

Some people thought about no one but themselves. They drove as though there was no one else on the road that mattered, and when they parked they evinced the same thoughtless attitude. In Butch's opinion some of this thoughtless behaviour was downright criminal in its potential.

He jerked the collar of his jacket higher around his neck and glanced over the forecourt to the hospital entrance. A stream of visitors was still leaving. The bus that catered for the elderly and the non-drivers had drawn up at the gateway and he heard the rhythmic swishing of its windshield wipers.

A man in a felt hat and gaberdine raincoat hurried out of the shadows and headed for the Ford parked in front of Butch's car.

'I'm sorry, Butch,' he said. 'I thought I would be gone in time to let you out.'

'Oh, that's okay,' Butch told him,

watching him finger for his keys and open the driving side door. The man slid in behind the wheel and drove off. He had been thin and appeared to be middle-aged. Butch settled behind the wheel of his own car and gave his wet jaws a wipe with a handkerchief. He wondered who the man was. He was sure he was neither a friend nor an acquaintance. But they had likely met in the hospital and exchanged greetings. Although, if such an incident had taken place, Butch Deely had no recollection of it.

There was a positive convoy of cars on the road into town. A few of the drivers behind him insisted on driving with their headlamps on full beam and the lights glinted on the wing and rear-view mirrors, contriving a dazzle that was hurtful and irritating.

Butch knew there was a roadside tavern up ahead and he decided to pull in there and have a beer and perhaps a couple of hotdogs. It would obviate the bother of making supper when he got home to the loneliness of the house on Willow Road. Since Mona had gone into hospital he had eaten most of his meals in taverns and cafés. She would have a fit if she knew the sort of diet he was on these days. But he missed her presence from the house terribly and he could not find the heart to emulate her cooking. He assured her he was eating as well as he ever did, and perhaps he was. But there was no comparison between his wife's cooking and the samples they dished up in cafés.

He signalled his intention to turn off the road in good time and came to a halt opposite the front of the tavern. No sooner had he alighted than another car drew in behind and the driver killed his lamps.

The tavern was pretty well crowded, but he found a spot at the end of the counter and ordered a beer and hotdog. He had just taken his first pull from the schooner and his first bite from the hotdog when a man in dripping raincoat pushed on to the stool beside him.

'Well, talk about coincidence,' he said in a cheerful voice. 'It's you again, Butch.'

'Hi,' Butch mumbled round a mouthful

of food. It was the man who had greeted him in the hospital parking area. 'Great minds think alike, huh?'

'So it seems,' the other laughed. He wore steel-rimmed spectacles that had moistened up and took them off to wipe them with a clean white handkerchief. With the spectacles off, Butch noticed that his eyes were small and prominent, and of a deep blue shade. He also noticed that the man was much younger than he had taken him to be at the outset.

Butch searched in his memory for a pigeon hole that might accommodate the stranger, but without success. He was of the opinion that the man really was a stranger to him. But then, again, he had the feeling that the face was vaguely familiar, and it might be one he had seen often enough without any positive registering of recognition. But what made the stranger think he knew him well enough to greet him on a first name basis?

He ordered coffee and a hamburger, and when they came he munched the hamburger with a ravenous appetite. At the end of his snack he produced a pack of cigarettes and offered Butch one.

'Thanks.' Butch decided that the moment had come to put a straight question. 'You've got the edge on me, mister. It's funny, but I can't remember your name. What is it?'

'My name is Alfred Jones.' His eyes twinkled behind the thick lenses of his spectacles. 'Surely you remember me, Butch. You live at Willow Road down in town, don't you?'

'Yeah, I do.'

'Well, I happen to live there as well. You live in number sixty-six, don't you?'

'That's right, I do.' Jones was smiling broadly as he talked. For all that, Butch was aware of a twinge of uneasiness. He was quite certain he had never seen Alfred Jones on Willow Road.

'I live in number twenty,' Jones said. 'That might explain it. We live at opposite ends of the street. But I've seen you leave your truck at the front door on several occasions. You drive for State-Wide trucking company?'

'I've been driving for them for close on fifteen years.'

'Fourteen years and three months to be exact,' Jones amended with that cheerful smile. 'Oh, don't be frightened or angry, Butch. I'm not a spy in any sense of the word. But I do happen to be a student of human nature. I take a keen interest in the people of whatever locality I happen to be living in.'

'I see,' Butch grunted, somewhat nonplussed. He bit into his second hotdog, discovering that the zest had faded from his own appetite. He wished he had driven straight home.

Jones ordered another hamburger and another cup of coffee. He offered Butch a second cigarette, but he indicated the one that remained untouched at his elbow. Butch swallowed his beer and struck a match to light the cigarette. He puffed for a moment in silence, hearing the loud buzz of conversation that swelled through the tavern.

Jones made short work of the hamburger and the cup of coffee.

'Your wife is expecting her first baby, Butch.'

It was a statement rather than a query

and Butch jerked on his stool. He felt like telling Jones to go away and pick on someone else to be the subject of his studies. But the man seemed harmless enough, and there was just the chance he was lonely and without any family ties of his own.

'That's right,' he said while his mobile mouth bent in a weak grin. 'Our very first kid. I just hope Mona would hurry up and have the kid.' He realized he was eager to have someone sympathetic to confide in. And if Jones was a neighbour who had taken an interest in him and Mona . . .

'Yes, the baby appears to be a trifle reluctant to step into this world of ours,' Jones said seriously. 'You know, Butch, I often wonder if it's right to bring children into such a world.'

'Now, wait a minute,' Butch cried while the short hairs at the nape of his neck bristled. 'What kind of stupid talk is that? If a couple want to have a kid why shouldn't they go ahead and have one? What's wrong with the world anyhow? The world is no worse and no better than it's ever been. You'd call the whole thing off and let the human race die a natural death?'

'Of course I wouldn't,' Jones said with a trace of asperity manifesting itself in his tone. 'But I do have definite ideas on the subject, Butch.'

'Yeah, so it seems,' Butch said gruffly. 'What kind of ideas do you have? You haven't got a family of your own?'

'No, I haven't.'

'Then it figures.' He could afford to feel sorry for Alfred Jones at this juncture. Perhaps there was something wrong with him or his wife and they couldn't have children. Butch knew a truckie who couldn't stand the sight of kids. One day a kid had kicked a ball into the roadway in front of his truck. When the kid came to fetch his ball the truckie had taken him by the scruff of the neck and warmed his ears. Butch had been passing at the time and had intervened.

'You keep your nose out of this, Deely. It isn't your kid, is it? Then keep your nose out of it.'

'But it might be my kid. It might be

your kid, Joe. Would you like a guy to thump your kid around the ears for kicking his ball into the road?'

'You haven't got a kid and neither have I, Deely. Little monsters they are. Little terrors. What about the mugging that's going on? Who's doing all the mugging — old guys of eighty?'

Later, Butch had learned that Joe's wife had lost two children at birth, and she had been told it was impossible to bring a live baby into the world.

Jones might have a similar bee in his hat.

'Are you married?' he asked Jones.

'No, I'm not married.'

That figured as well, Butch decided. Then Jones might be possessed with a kink that had twisted his outlook.

'So you live at Willow Road all on your own? That can't be a lot of fun for you, Alfred.'

Jones laughed easily, apparently genuinely amused. It seemed he could make a guess regarding what Butch was thinking.

'Don't run away with the notion that I'm a woman-hater or a misanthrope,

Butch. Or that I have anything against children. In fact, it's because I love them so much that I'm against bringing them into this cruel, uncivilized world.'

To Butch's way of thinking what Jones had just stated would be funny if it wasn't so tragic. What could be better for a man and woman than having a kid to call their son? What experience could equal that of watching him growing up and becoming a man himself, guiding him and teaching him so that he would be equipped to cope with life?

'So you don't like the state of the world, Alfred. Well, I'm inclined to agree with you that it isn't perfect. So we shouldn't have children until it is perfect? Is that what you're really trying to say?'

'I'm trying to say this,' Jones explained patiently, 'not enough time and energy are devoted by the people of the world to the task of making it perfect.'

'For pete's sake, Mr Jones! A perfect world? Who ever heard of a perfect world? Who ever heard of a perfect town, a perfect community?'

'Exactly,' Jones nodded sagely. 'Who

ever heard of a perfect community? But it isn't outside the realms of feasibility to endeavour to make a community so. Would you agree with that, Butch?'

'Well, I — Look, Mr Jones, it seems to me that you get a kick out of riding this hobby horse. Would it be too impertinent to ask you what you're doing to make the world or the community you live in a better place for kids to live?'

'I'm doing my best,' Jones told him with startling candour.

'You are! More power to your elbow then. Are you in welfare work or something of the sort, Alfred?'

'Something of the sort, Butch. So you would be in favour of helping to make the world a better place to live in?'

'Of course I would? Who wouldn't?' Butch lighted the cigarette he had given him and puffed. He saw no reason why he shouldn't humour Jones. He was a harmless crank even if there were some aspects of his philosophy that jarred. 'But what could I do to help?' he asked with a dry chuckle. 'I fill in a pretty full day as it is. I don't have much spare time at the minute — what with Mona being in hospital and all.'

'I understand,' Jones smiled. 'I understand perfectly, Butch. By the way, have you got another dog yet? I believe your last dog was run down by an automobile and killed.'

'Yeah, it was. But here . . . That happened two years ago. You haven't been in town that long?'

'Oh, I've been here for longer than you imagine, Butch. I saw a handsome dog in a pet-shop the other day — '

'Not for me, thanks,' Butch broke in on him. 'Mona thought the world of Rover. She wouldn't have another dog about the place.'

'There you are then. A question of sentiment.' He buttoned up his raincoat and prepared to leave. The crowd in the tavern was thinning out. Jones laid his hand on Butch's shoulder in a friendly gesture. 'Good-bye for now, Butch. I'll see you around.'

'Sure,' Butch muttered, staring after him until he vanished into the rain-swept darkness. He sat on for a while, wondering about Alfred Jones and his queer talk. The more he thought of the stranger the more baffled he became at the amount of his history he had garnered. But to what end? What the devil was he really driving at? Why was he so interested in him and Mona?

Finally Butch concluded that Jones must be some kind of nut and it would be best to ignore him and his screwy ideas.

2

The following day proved a particularly busy one for Butch, so that he had little time to think about Alfred Jones, even if he had felt inclined to reflect on the stranger and his odd talk of last night.

He did think a lot about his wife, Mona, in hospital, though, and he put two calls through to County Hospital to inquire how she was. He received the expected stock answer from whoever took the calls. Mrs Deely was comfortable and there was no change in her condition.

It was almost six o'clock before he and his helper got back to the depot at the end of the last fifty-mile journey of the day. They left the truck in the maintenance bay for its nightly check-over and parted at the gate, Pete Rawlins driving off in his three-year-old Volvo towards the south end of town and Butch setting out at top speed for Willow Road to grab a quick snack and shower and dress.

He worked so swiftly he was out of the house again at six forty-five on the dot. It was a warm evening and he wore an open-necked shirt and his tan, lightweight tweed sport coat. He had just tooled the Olds to the end of the driveway when he saw Jones.

There he was, smiling broadly, his blue eyes twinkling behind the lenses of his glasses. He had a bunch of beautiful cream and white roses in a plastic envelope and he raised the roses in an indication of wanting Butch to stop.

'For your wife, Butch,' he suggested with an eagerness that reminded Butch of a kid wanting to bum a ride to the end of the block on his truck. 'Do you think she'll like them?'

'But, Alfred — Mr Jones — you shouldn't. It's altogether too much from a total stranger.'

'A total stranger? Oh, come, come, Butch. We aren't strangers to each other by any weird stretch of the imagination. Do you like them yourself?'

'I'll say I do. They're wonderful. I bet they've got loads of fragrance. I bring flowers to Mona only on Sundays. Well, I don't have the time to — '

'Of course. You're a busy man, Butch. I won't delay you. Please give my kind regards to your good lady.'

'I'll certainly do that, Alfred. Thanks a million.'

'My pleasure, Butch.'

What a queer bird to be sure, Butch thought as he drove on to the end of the street. But he was quite harmless, really. Lonesome and friendless. That was it. He was merely seeking a little human contact and friendship.

Butch glanced in the rear-view mirror and was surprised when he failed to see any sign of Jones. Certainly he could not have walked back home to number twenty in that short space of time. He had not appeared in his car as there had been no other traffic at the kerb when he drove out.

Butch shrugged and smiled faintly. The mysterious Alfred Jones, he reflected. A mixed-up oddball who wanted to make the world a better place for kids to grow up in. It would be something to discuss with Mona at her bedside in the hospital. Sometimes they ran out of mundane fuel for conversation and sat looking at each other, feeling awkward in their longing for each other's comfort. He glanced at the bouquet of roses now and smiled again. It was an extremely nice gesture by the stranger in number twenty.

Mona had more colour in her cheeks this evening, he fancied, kissing her on the brow and placing the roses on the bedside locker. She had to open them immediately and sniff them.

'Roses! Beautiful . . . I love the scent of roses, Butch. But, do you know something? You can't go on smelling them and enjoying the scent. It's the first sniff that counts, isn't it? You've got to wait a little while before smelling them again. I'll ask the nurse to put them in water. But where did you get roses so early in the year, Butch? They must have cost.'

'Not a dime,' he said smugly. 'A guy came along the street as I was leaving the house and gave them to me. He also sent his regards to accompany them.'

'You've got to be joking! But give me

three guesses to decide who is our generous neighbour. Not Mr Midgley?'

'Not Mr Midgley, honey. Try again. He did ask me this morning how you were coming along, though. So did Mr Krantz and Mr Hornbeck.'

'Not Mr Krantz and not Mr Hornbeck? Then I'm afraid I must give up, darling. That just about exhausts the possibilities that spring readily to mind.'

'Mr Jones,' he told her and waited for her reaction. Mona's reaction was a slight frown and a drawing of her underlip between her teeth.

'Mr Jones — I'm sorry, darling. That name doesn't ring a bell. I'm sure I know the name of everyone on Willow Road. He must be a stranger to the street.'

'Not according to Mr Jones, honey. His full name is Alfred Jones. He lives at number twenty, he tells me. And according to the dope he has on us and me in particular, he's been in the district for quite a long time.'

'Number twenty, Willow Road? You're sure of that, Butch?'

'He told me, didn't he? He might be a

24

bit of an oddball, but I wouldn't call him a brazen liar and I can't label him as being ungenerous. You mean to say you've never heard of him?'

There was a faint ring of uneasiness in Butch's voice.

'I never have,' Mona declared, taking his fingers in her own and fondling each one in turn. She gave a short laugh. 'Why, I remember now, Butch. Number twenty is empty. It's been empty for three years, almost. Are you forgetting that little woman who used to take a poodle around on a lead? Remember what I used to sing when she went past the front? That old song. 'Little old lady passing by' . . . '

'Mrs Consby!' Butch gulped. 'Yeah, I remember her, honey. Did she live in number twenty?'

'Of course she did. Then she just packed her things one day and left. Since then the house has been empty. Wait a minute! There's a 'For Sale' notice in the front yard unless I'm mistaken. Yes, there is. It was there up to a few weeks ago.'

Butch paled somewhat and fumbled for his cigarettes. He pulled himself together in time and rubbed the hard angle of his jaw instead. He could feel those short hairs prickling at the nape of his neck.

'But who's Alfred Jones then?' he asked hoarsely. 'Why would he say he's living in number twenty if it's a lie? Look, he was in the hospital last night, Mona. He parked his car in a line with the front of ours. I was thinking what a thoughtless creep he was when he showed up and greeted me.'

Mona laughed again. She retrieved his fingers.

'He greeted you by name?'

'Yeah, he did. The way he spoke he seemed to know me from way back. But I let it ride and he drove off to let me out. Then I pulled in at Wetzer's tavern for a beer, and who should come in and take a stool beside me at the counter?'

'Mr Jones?'

'You win the cocoa-nut, baby. I tried to take it in my stride. He asked how you were. He knew you were expecting a baby and that the baby is overdue. He knew I was working for the trucking company. He actually knew to the exact month the length of time I've been with State-Wide.'

This revelation caused Mona's eyes to widen in horror.

'He must be an investigator of some kind, Butch. You know, one of those snoopers who pry into the affairs of people who owe money.'

'But we don't owe money, for heaven's sake. No more than the average John Doe owes for some trifling thing or another.'

'What about your job itself, darling?' Mona suggesed as the idea occurred to her. 'If he knows so much about us and the length of time you've been with State-Wide, perhaps he's someone employed by the trucking company to keep track of its employees.'

Yes, it might be something worthy of chewing on, Butch realized. But he dismissed the notion promptly.

'That's out for a start, sweetie. If Jones worked for State-Wide and was bent on prying into my business he'd be the last person to admit he knows so much about me. There has to be another answer. And he doesn't strike you like a snoop. He's got this bee in his hat, you see . . . '

'What bee? Not about me, surely! But he did send me flowers, Butch.' She reddened and he could sense that she was casting into her memory. 'I don't know any Alfred Jones,' she said firmly and with an edge of challenge to her tone.

'Hold on. Hold on. I'm not going to fly off in a jealous panic. I'm not saying he's getting at you in a roundabout fashion. I'm not saying he's got any ulterior motives at all.'

'But he does have this bee . . . '

Butch chuckled at her expression. He longed for a cigarette but he would have to wait until he left the hospital. In a light-hearted manner he related all that had taken place between him and the stranger in Wetzer's tavern. At the end of the recital Mona lay back on her pillows and laughed softly.

'He talked like that? He wants to turn the world on its head and keep the birth-rate static until his wonderful world is an actual reality? He would like to recruit your services to the cause? Oh, Butch, he's a crank, of course. A harmless crank, maybe, but a crank nevertheless.'

'I guess he must be,' Butch conceded with a grin. 'But he did send you roses so we'll bear with him. All the same, I can't get over him saying he's living at number twenty. I know what I'll do. I'll drive past the house on the way home and have a gander at it. Just out of curiosity. Well, he could be squatting in the house and the authorities don't know that he is. Even so, I couldn't find the heart to give the guy away . . . Say, let's forget Alfred for a while and concentrate on us. Us and this kid you're keeping under cover. Did the medico say when — '

'Wait a minute, Butch,' Mona interrupted him, clutching his hand. 'You said that Mr Jones was visiting at the hospital here last night. You said that?'

'There's no doubt about it. He had parked his car in front of mine, like I told you. He came out of the hospital, and — Yeah, I get the message, honey. If he doesn't have any friends or relations, who was he visiting with?'

'He didn't say who?'

'Not a word. He said practically nothing about himself, apart from giving throat to his screwy notions on the state of the world and what he would like to do about it. But he's bound to know somebody in town if he's been here for so long. A friend or a casual acquaintance. Hey, hold on,' Butch choked as still another idea flashed in on him. 'Get a load of this, Mona. Jones drove out of the hospital grounds in front of me last night. I'm dead sure of that. He took the road leading down to town. There was a positive stream of traffic on the road, so that we must have been well separated when I set off. Then — then how come he drove in behind me at the tavern? He said something about it being a coincidence. Would you call that a coincidence?'

Almost as soon as he said this he regretted the anxious outburst. Mona paled and laid a hand on her full bosom. Her eyes reflected a growing concern.

'You're absolutely certain?' she whispered.

'Well, nearly,' Butch said weakly in an attempt to mend a little of the damage. 'But I could have made a mistake, I guess. Oh, to the devil with Jones, sweetie. Let's drop it, shall we? Let's talk about you and the kid. No!' he said sternly when Mona's lips formed words to pursue the subject. 'No more of Jones tonight, honey. You've got enough to think of without worrying about a screwball with some sort of fixation . . . '

★ ★ ★

Finally, Butch kissed his wife good-bye and took his leave of her. They parted on a note of gaiety, Butch having regaled her with a description of the frills he had added to the proposed nursery and subsequent rumpus room. On his way out he had a good mind to see the medico in charge and put the query straight to him when he could expect his wife to give birth to the baby. His worry in this respect had been allayed somewhat when Mona said she felt one or two twinges of pain this morning. But even so, he felt that the business was dragging interminably.

The doctors were usually occupied with one thing or another this late in the evening, so he would wait until tomorrow and put a phone call through to the hospital, demanding to have a word with the chief medical officer.

Darkness had fallen by now and the sky was lit up with a million twinkling stars. Butch walked to his Olds, half-expecting to hear Alfred Jones greet him. Of course Jones had not intended visiting at the hospital this evening. Otherwise he would not have been waiting at the Deelys' front entrance with the roses.

Nevertheless, Butch walked rapidly to his parked car, seated himself behind the wheel, and drove away swiftly. He cut out in front of another automobile which was entitled to the right of way and drew an angry horn bleep for his discourtesy.

A film of sweat layered his brow as he was forced to slow his speed of travel to suit the flow of traffic worming back towards town. When the lights of Wetzer's tavern showed up ahead he flashed his indicator and eased over to the parking area. Alighting, he eyed the traffic worm crawling past, as though challenging Alfred Jones to repeat his performance of

32

the previous night. Of course there was no sign of Jones' Ford and he lighted a cigarette before entering the tavern.

The first person his eyes fell on was Jones at the counter.

At that instant Butch felt a snaking of cold fear in the region of his spine. It was too much of a coincidence that the stranger should have come here again tonight. Too much of a coincidence that he should have stopped off here again tonight. How many times in the past had he halted at the tavern on his journey home to Caldwell from the hospital? Three times in all. It had been touch and go whether he stopped off for a drink tonight.

Had some strange force impelled him to halt at the bar, to go in and join the stranger sitting there calmly and munching at a hamburger?

'I'd better get a grip on myself,' he muttered fiercely. 'This guy could drive me round the loop before I know it.'

He decided to insert himself between two other customers at the near end of the bar. But, as though Jones had received secret intimation of his presence, he turned his head at that moment and smiled benignly at Butch.

'Oh, hello again, Butch. Fancy meeting you here. Come and join me.'

Butch's first impulse was to ignore the invitation and make it plain to Jones that he was giving him the brush-off. Then he reflected that this would be tantamount to surrendering to the uneasiness that gripped him and giving credence to the fantastic supposition that Jones was really something out of the ordinary.

There was a vacant stool beside the stranger and he eased himself on to it. Jones' eyes glinted mildly through the lenses of his spectacles. He had finished eating his hamburger and began wiping his hands daintily with a handkerchief. His whole easy-going manner made nonsense of the wild ideas churning inside Butch's head. Even so, he was determined to be on guard and to dissect every word uttered by the other.

'And how is Mrs Deely tonight?' was the stranger's gentle preamble. 'In good health, I trust?'

'Yeah, Mona is doing fine, Alfred. She sends her thanks for the roses you gave me.'

'No thanks are necessary, Butch. Are you hungry?' He raised a finger to attract one of the busy counter men.

'No, I just came in for a beer. Look, I'll pay for my own beer, if you don't mind, Alfred.'

'By all means!' Jones laughed and it had the effect of making Butch's hasty objection sound silly. 'A man likes to be independent of others. It's a highly laudable ambition, my friend. Yes, a highly laudable ambition.'

The use of the term 'friend' set Butch's hackles up on edge. He ordered a beer and when it came he took a hefty swallow from the schooner Jones had a cigarette pack in his hand and offered him one.

'No, thanks, Alfred. I've smoked all I need to smoke for one day. I'm trying to cut them down, you see.'

'Yes, I've been trying to cut them down myself,' Jones confided whimsically. 'But once you get hooked on them — if that is the word — the habit is very hard to abandon. Nothing fresh on the expected new arrival? I'm sure your impatience is beginning to get the better of you, Butch.'

'You can say that again.' Butch laid his drink down and rubbed his lips with the back of his hand. He said soberly, 'It's an odd thing, Mr Jones, but my wife has no recollection of you living on our street. Do you know her at all?'

Jones' blue eyes twinkled behind his glasses.

'Do I know her? My dear boy, of course I know her. I know her almost as well as I know you, as I know everyone else who lives in the district . . . '

He looked smug when he said that. He expressed amazement as well at the idea of Butch not being fully aware of his knowledge.

'But how can you? I mean, Mona doesn't know you. I described you to her, but it made no difference. She's never even heard of a man living at Willow Road called Jones. You really do live on Willow Road, Alfred?'

'That's where I live, Butch. Dear, dear! I never suggested that your wife was acquainted with me. I'm sure I've passed her on the street a hundred times and she never gave me a second glance. The same might be said of the other residents in the locality. They seldom if ever notice me. In fact, I might not be living there at all for the attention I get.'

'I see,' Butch muttered. Then they could be wrong about Jones and he really was one of those people who had the knack of being anonymous to the point where they might not exist. That he was an eccentric there was no doubt, so why should an eccentric not bother to remove or cause to have removed the 'For Sale' sign in the front yard of his house? He finished off his drink and rose, grinning at Jones. He explained that he had had a tiring day driving his truck and felt bushed. He might run into Jones again soon and have another chat.

'Don't worry on that score, Butch. You'll be seeing plenty of me in future.'

3

Butch Deely's cold sweat lasted until he had arrived at the end of the street that was called Willow Road. Once upon a time there had been two rows of willow trees in the street, but several years back workmen had come along to lay new pipes under the surface of the road, and the line of trees on the west side of the street had been sacrificed to hygiene and progress. The row which continued to grow unmolested was on the Deelys' side of the street and flourished despite the havoc wrought by exhaust fumes from automobiles and lawn mowers, and the divers varieties of weed-killers and fertilizers utilized by over-enthusiastic gardeners.

One of those trees grew alongside the entrance drive leading to the doorway of number sixty-six, and during the years Butch had come to have a fondness for this tree. It waved good-bye to him like an old friend in the mornings and was the first landmark he looked for on returning home in the evenings.

Tonight there was something wrong with his tree.

Butch brought the Olds to a halt at the curb, remembering that he had intended driving past number twenty to see whether the 'For Sale' continued to dominate the weeds in the front yard. That front yard had always been thick with weeds. Mrs Consby could quite easily have asked a man to chop the weeds down for her, but she was against anyone interfering with the weeds. They had been put there for a purpose, just as wild flowers and other plants had been put there for a purpose. There was every bit as much true beauty and grace in a weed as there was in any flower, provided that you were equipped with the talent to appreciate the fact.

It was funny how so many forgotten memories of Mrs Consby should filter back when you began to concentrate. Yes, there was certainly a lot more to the human mind than the average person imagined there was.

Then Butch's gaze lifted to the willow tree and he emitted a low whistle of surprise. What the devil *had* happened to that tree? Or was it simply that the shadows were playing tricks on him? There were only two lamp standards situated on Willow Road — one at the north end and one at the south end, with the result that at night the shadows had a ball.

Butch killed the motor and leaped out of the Olds to investigate. The next instant he uttered a soft oath. A large branch appeared to have split close to the main trunk and was trailing forlornly across the blacktop drive. Butch forgot all else in his anxiety for the tree. He loved trees and forests, and quailed when he saw television programmes showing how the northern forests were being massacred in the interests of providing people with next month's or next year's edition of their favourite newspaper.

'I bet some skunk kid was swinging on that when he got my back turned.' He remembered the kid his wife was about to have and softened considerably. 'No, a kid wouldn't do that, I guess. There's nothing but good kids on this street. Maybe there was rot in the wood that I never noticed.'

He went back to the car to take his flashlight from the glove compartment, but even when he shone it directly at the place where the branch had split away he couldn't really determine how the split had occurred.

'I'll get the ladder from the garage,' he grunted, making for the small building at the side of the house and emerging presently with a twelve-foot aluminium ladder. He placed the ladder against the main trunk of the tree and climbed. A minute later he had the beam of the flashlight trained on the spot where the branch had broken free. 'No rot at all!' he marvelled. 'Now, how in hell did that happen if the tree is healthy?'

Indeed, it looked as though the branch had been broken away cleanly by the sheer brute strength of a mighty hand. A saw could not have made a better job of it, but there was absolutely no trace of saw teeth having been fretting at the wood.

'What are you doing up there, Butch?'

The suddenness and unexpectedness of the voice caused Butch to lose his balance fractionally, and had he not made a quick grab for a slender branch overhead he would have toppled to the asphalt facing of the drive. For several seconds he was unable to do anything other than glare down venomously at Alfred Jones.

He had not heard the stranger's approach, and he must have crept up on him on tiptoes to get here so quietly.

'Oh, it's you, Alfred,' he said hoarsely, and added with a leakage of his temper, 'How the devil did you get here so quickly?'

'Quickly, Butch? Be careful now,' he hastened, gripping the ladder rail and holding it until Butch descended to stand beside him. 'But I left the tavern on your heels. Didn't you hear me speaking to you as you got into your car?'

'No, I didn't.' Butch's tone remained rough, but he saw the silliness in losing his head over a trifle. 'That tree,' he went on, rubbing sweat from his brow with the back of his hand. 'It was fine when I left home to go to the hospital. Look at it now.'

'A branch has broken,' Jones observed in amusement. 'But the broken branch of a tree is hardly something to be worked up about?'

'Yeah, I guess you're right.' He laughed without humour, peering round to see if there was a car parked nearby. There was no car there but the Olds. 'It's just — Well, it's just a tree after all.'

'Exactly, Butch. They say trees have brains and feelings and emotions. Do you know that some people treat all forms of plant life with the same reverence they treat human life?'

'Yeah, so I've heard.' The evening was still warm, but Butch was aware of a decided coolness in the region of his spine. The lenses of Jones's spectacles glinted in the feeble lighting. He brought cigarettes from the pocket of his raincoat and extended one to Butch. Butch shook his head.

'I'm trying to cut them down.'

'Yes, I remember. You said so, Butch.' He gave a dry chuckle. 'You'll have to cut that branch down as well.'

'You bet I will. I'll fetch the saw from the toolshed.'

He half-turned away from Jones, then paused and ran his tongue across his lips.

'Look, Alfred, there's no one at home. I've got a couple of bottles in the fridge. Another bottle in the cupboard. Would you care — '

'Thanks all the same, Butch. No, I'll have to buzz off. It's time I was making out my re — ' There he stopped speaking and laughed, as if discretion had put a curb on his tongue. He waved his hand and passed on along the street. He hummed to himself as he went, a man, apparently, at peace with himself and the neighbourhood, if not with the world in general.

Butch went round the back of the garage to reach the toolshed, using the flashlight to find what he wanted. The bulb in the light socket was fused and he must remember to replace it. He was glad he had invited Jones to step into his house for a drink. The invitation had served a twofold purpose: he had proved to himself that he was not frightened of Jones, and he had proved to Jones that at heart he was a friendly and generous guy.

'But why do I have to prove I'm not scared?' he muttered angrily. 'Why do I have to prove I'm all heart? What the hell is it about that joker that makes me feel I'm spitting on my grave?' He nearly said something then he might have regretted later. 'It's time I was making out my re — ' It's time he was making out what? Report? Reports? What the devil has he got to report on? Who is he going to report to? I just wonder if he's some kind of snoop after all? Would he be setting me up for some kind of fall? But in the interests of what, for pete's sake?

Butch climbed the ladder again with the saw and lopped off the trailing limbs that supported the broken branch. He trailed the branch round to the back yard and left it against the fence dividing his garden and yard from the one next door. That done he replaced the saw in the toolshed and drove his car in from the street.

He let himself into the house and

helped himself to a bottle of beer from the fridge. He settled down before the TV in the living-room and switched on to catch the late race and football results. Then he thought of Jones and that sign in his front yard and leaned over to switch the TV off.

He placed a cigarette between his lips and lighted it in the gloom of the street. An automobile came in from the north end of Willow Road and headed for the south end at a smart lick. He recognized the new Pontiac that Phil Pentecost had bought lately. Pentecost was a travelling salesman who was supposed to be making a load. There were rumours in the air that he was moving out of Willow Road soon to a new swank development in the southern suburbs of Caldwell. Anyhow, good luck to Pentecost and all who sailed with him. Free enterprise and the validity of aspiration were what democracy was all about.

The street was quiet now and Butch walked at a leisurely gait. To anyone who saw him he was just that trucker from along the road whose wife was in hospital expecting a baby. Likely he was taking a stroll in the night air to calm his nerves.

He ticked off the numbers of the houses mentally, feeling a pulse of excitement beating in his veins as he drew closer to number twenty. There it was, only four houses away now. Yes, the sign was standing in the front yard as Mona had said it was. What kind of crazy goat was this Alfred Jones? Did he want to kid folks along that the house remained unoccupied?

Butch walked past the driveway leading to the front door of the house and continued for a dozen yards; then he swung back, walking even slower than before. Common sense told him to forget all about Alfred Jones and head home for bed. He knew how he felt in the mornings when the alarm went off and he awoke with the convictions that he could sleep for a month. It would be like that in the morning. He might even dream about the stranger with the bright blue eyes and the penchant for presenting roses to pregnant women. Small wonder if he did. But why had Jones said he was living at number twenty when it was obvious that the house was empty?

Yes, Butch was sure the house was empty. The front windows were drab and scummy, crying out for a good wash-down and clean. There were no curtains on those front windows, no shades in place.

Butch fingered the flashlight he had pushed into his jacket pocket and glanced around him. As far as he could make out there was no one paying any attention to him. In any case, who would comment on or object to that truck driver having a look at the empty dwelling? He might know someone who was interested in buying it: one of his pals at work, perhaps.

Butch brought his teeth together and strode up the shadowy driveway to reach the door. There was one effective method of calling Jones' bluff. He would simply thumb the bell push and see what happened. In the event of the stranger opening the door to him he would make some excuse. What? Normally cool and not lacking talent for improvisation, just then Butch's brain wanted to be an uncaring jumble. If he would admit to the truth he was more than a trifle frightened of Alfred Jones. Not frightened of him in any physical sense. And perhaps frightened was not the correct word. Jones made him uneasy, unsure of himself. He made him think of things that were better left alone in the dim, dark well that was part of every man's mind.

In a spasm of fierce reaction Butch pressed the faded ivorine button.

The chimes of the bell came faintly to his ears, but the sound was loud enough to tell him the bell was working. And, Jones, if he actually lived in the house and was engaged in making out his report or whatever it was he had wanted to do, could not fail to hear it.

Another car came into Willow Road from the south end. It cruised down the street and turned at a driveway on the opposite side of the road. The motor died and a car door was slammed. Then silence and Butch could almost hear the thumping of his heart against his ribcage.

No sign of Alfred Jones. No scuffle of feet in the hallway behind the door. Butch could visualize the layout of the house: all of the houses on the street had been erected to a single pattern. Off the main hall was the sitting-room, below that the minor hallway leading to the bedrooms. The kitchen was at the rear of the house, but even if Jones was in there, making coffee or a meal, he could hear the bell clearly.

Butch rang again.

Two minutes later he was ready to retreat to his own home. Jones was a liar of the first water, but whatever reason he had for lying he could keep it to himself. Butch didn't want to know about it. From now on he would see to it that Alfred Jones was kept at arm's length. He had no further use for the man. Not a liar. Not a deceitful crank.

Then Butch's curiosity got the better of him. He left the front door and went along the side of the garage to gain the rear. There was no light at the rear of the building either. The back yard was weeded over and gave off a sickly sweet smell. A plastic bucket was lying, upside down, in the dirt. Not far away a spade was lying by a clutter of shrubbery.

Butch retraced his steps to the front, stopping at the garage and testing the door. The door swung open and he saw that the garage was empty. Wherever Alfred Jones had parked his Ford he had not parked it here. But perhaps he had gone off to make a call on someone. Yes, that could be it.

Butch brought the flashlight from his pocket and fingered the switch. He swept the thin beam over the walls, the ceiling of the garage. The place was as clean as a new pin. Seldom, if ever, had a car been housed here. Of course, Mrs Consby had not been a car owner, so that would explain the comparative neatness of everything.

Yet, Butch's keen sense of smell told him that exhaust fumes skulked in the corners. The garage had been used recently for holding a car.

He played the beam of the flashlight on the floor now and saw several dark spots that glistened in the yellow glow. He stooped and touched one of the spots with a fingertip. Engine oil without doubt.

The prickling sensation touched the nape of his neck.

He hurried to the open and closed the large door behind him, doing it gently so that there would be no tell-tale squeaking of the hinges. He had an urge to head back along the street as fast as he could go. But his curiosity was growing in proportion with his anxiety. He knew he would lie awake, thinking of the house, wondering if a man could be living there, if Jones could be living there. Wondering what his game was.

He stepped through a tangle of weeds to gain the front window and cupped his hands about his eyes to peer into the room. The room beyond the window was absolutely bare — no furnishings of any description, no carpet or rug on the floor. Nothing.

So Alfred Jones was a squatter after all, he thought grimly. Perhaps he was using only one room of the house to sleep in and live in. If it were possible to break in and see . . .

Butch walked to the driveway entrance and glanced up and down the street. The street was deserted, hushed under the shadowed stillness of late evening. Then he heard the faint scratch of canned laughter emerging from some TV in a neighbouring house.

Butch retraced his steps yet again, ending up at the front door of the house. He knew that a number of the houses in the street had similar locks despite what a buyer was told to the contrary on taking possession. On one occasion Mrs Hornbecker had mislaid her doorkey and Mona had offered to try their key in the lock. Much to their amazement the key had fitted.

His key in hand, Butch leaned his weight slightly against the door panel and gaped when the door eased inwards.

'Holy smoke! The door wasn't locked. This really must prove that Jones is a squatter. He must have forced the lock when he decided to camp here at the beginning . . . '

Pulse racing, Butch entered the hallway and went along it gingerly. The floor underneath gave off gentle creaks of protest. There was no need to use his flashlight to find his way around as he knew the layout of the compartments by heart.

The living-room really was empty and badly in need of airing. It reeked of fustiness and neglect. Butch closed the door and continued. He examined the bedrooms next, expecting to find a bed or bunk in one of them, and perhaps a chair and table. But no, the same lack of furnishings persisted. Where then did Jones sleep at night? Where did he sit down to eat? Was he living in the house at all?

Butch was forced to the conclusion that the house known as number twenty Willow Road was uninhabited and had been so for a very long time.

With more boldness now, Butch proceeded to the kitchen, seeing the empty shelves, the vacant cupboards. There was no trace of a table or chair. Not even a spoon was to be found in the cutlery drawer. Strange. Or was it so strange? It depended on whether you were prepared to believe one word that issued from the lips of Alfred Jones.

Alfred Jones was a crank with bells on. A downright liar to boot. A phoney. But why did he have to pick on Butch Deely? That soft-spoken talk. That tear-jerking philosophy. Those beautiful roses . . .

Suddenly Butch heard something and froze. The sound — whatever it was and whatever was responsible for it — appeared to be coming from the other side of the kitchen door. It consisted of a low rhythmic clicking or tapping; then there was a series of faint bleeps that reminded Butch of an automobile horn being sounded in the distance.

But how could the noise be coming from the area beyond the kitchen doorway? There was nothing out there but the weeded back yard, those forlorn bushes, the plastic bucket and the spade.

Butch Deely felt the blood pounding in his ears. An alarm bell was jangling wildly at the back of his brain. Get out of here, his instinct told him. Get out of here fast while the going is good.

Nuts, Butch thought to himself, wiping sweat from his brow in an abstracted motion. Whatever was making those sounds he intended to see it. For all he knew, Alfred Jones could be some kind of spy who was using the empty house as a base for his operations. If that was so he was duty-bound to investigate and to turn over the results of his investigation to the proper authorities.

Butch's hand gripped the door knob and twisted. He pushed the door slowly open, hearing those clickings and tappings and bleepings growing louder. He peered through and saw a long, low-ceilinged chamber. There was no one in the chamber, but against one wall a bank of instrument panels was located that flickered and tapped and clicked in steady rhythm.

With a hoarse cry Butch slammed the door and retreated, making for the front door in a shambling run.

4

He never stopped running until he had gained the entrance to his own driveway. There he dragged to a halt and leaned against the willow tree for several moments until his heart-beat slackened and he could breathe more normally.

His first impulse was to make for his next-door neighbour's house and blurt out the story to Andy Midgley. Midgley was a solid, down-to-earth type, and would help him regain his equilibrium and sense of perspective.

But no, it might be a mistake to inform Andy Midgley or anyone else in the street of his discovery. If a spy-ring of any description was operating in the district the police should be the first people to know about it. The F.B.I., really. But how to get in touch with the F.B.I. without making contact with the police?

Butch was heading for his car when he had another change of mind. It wasn't necessary to drive to police headquarters in order to raise the alarm; he could do it by telephone. He took his key from his jacket pocket with trembling fingers and inserted it in the door lock. Inside, he slammed the door and put his shoulders against the wood panel, bracing them, striving to bring a single grain of common sense to bear.

Wait a minute, he told himself. How could that chamber be attached to the rear of Jones' house, granting that it really was the headquarters of Alfred Jones. It was impossible for that chamber to be attached to the rest of the house. He had been round at the rear and he had seen what was there. Certainly there was no extension jutting from the main structure.

'I must be going nuts. I must be slipping my gears . . . That damned Jones! Why couldn't he stay away from me? What the hell does he want of me?'

Butch shuddered, knowing a kind of fear he had never before experienced in his life. Whatever the true situation consisted of, there was something out of focus at number twenty Willow Road.

Badly out of focus. He would be shirking his duty as a responsible citizen if he failed to inform the police, and that immediately.

Butch thrust on through to the living-room and slumped down on a chair by the phone. He had the receiver in his hand when he realized that he had no idea of the number of police headquarters. He would have to look it up in the book. No, he could call the operator at the exchange and have her connect him.

Butch dialled and worked a cigarette to his lips while he waited. The operator came on, her voice calm with sanity.

'Caldwell exchange. What can I do for you?'

'Put me through to the police,' Butch said in a tone he scarcely recognized. 'Do it fast, will you.'

'Just a moment, sir. You mean the local police?'

'Of course I do. I — '

'Please let me have your name and address, sir.'

What the hell, Butch thought. So she's bound to know who's calling. When did he ever have to identify himself to get a connection?

'Butch — I mean Delmer Deely. I'm calling from my home. Number sixty-six Willow Road.'

'Please hold on.'

Butch tugged a match from his pocket and scraped it alight on the sole of his shoe. He was puffing hungrily when a flat voice spoke to him.

'Police Headquarters in Caldwell. Go ahead.'

'Look,' Butch blurted, 'could you send someone here as soon as possible?' He added rapidly, 'I'm Delmer Deely and I reside at sixty-six Willow Road. This is important.'

'All right, Mr Deely. Could you give me a clue regarding the nature of the trouble? There is trouble?'

'You send someone here to my house and he'll find out,' Butch snapped and hung up the receiver.

He left the living-room and went into the kitchen. His thoughts were full of Mona now, Mona and the kid she should be having any time. He wished Mona had

60

got over her confinement. He wished with a savage fervency that she were here right now to talk to him, to assure him that he actually was sane and in possession of all his faculties.

'But calm down,' he muttered to himself as he brought a can of beer from the fridge and tore it open. 'You are sane and there's no chance of you becoming a raving looney. Alfred Jones is the looney if there has to be one in the act. But no, he's not, by heaven! Jones is a crafty, conniving so-and-so. A foreign agent, maybe, planning to sabotage our democratic system . . . All that guff about making the world a better place to live in! Don't bring babies into such a cruel world! What the hell does that four-eyed punk know about it? What does he know about anything other than his cunning schemings?'

He drank the beer off and threw the empty can into the trash bin. He still felt thirsty and opened another can of beer. He drank this more slowly and lighted a fresh cigarette. He began pacing the floor of the living-room, fighting with his nervous agitation and desperately willing himself to be calm.

He was fumbling for still another cigarette when the doorbell rang. Butch hurried into the hall to open the door. He saw two uniformed officers gazing in at him.

'Delmer Deely?'

'That's me.' Butch mustered a grin, but it hurt his facial muscles and he let it go. 'You guys better come in a minute.'

They followed him into the living-room, eyes narrowed in suspicious alertness. They seemed surprised to find no one in the house but himself.

'All right, Deely,' the heavier built officer said gruffly, fingering his cleft chin. 'What's the jig? You didn't just call the cops to help you find the aspirin to cure your hang-over?'

'Look, I've got no hangover,' Butch retorted. His legs felt weak and he lowered himself to a chair. He gestured for the police officers to seat themselves, also.

They exchanged looks and stood where they were.

'Time's a wasting, bud. What is it? Why can't you get it off your chest?'

Butch swallowed hard and met the concerted scepticism in their unwavering eyes.

'It's like this,' he began and paused. 'Where do I start? I'd better tell you about Jones first of all, I guess.'

'Maybe you'd better,' the one with the cleft chin urged cynically. He inclined his head slightly and his fellow officer produced a notepad and ballpen. 'Now, who's Jones and where does he fit into it? And what exactly is he supposed to fit into?'

'He's a fellow I met. A stranger. But he says he's living at number twenty . . . '

'Oh, yeah?' The lighter built one of the pair scribbled something. 'Number twenty, where?'

'Hell, on Willow Road here, where else?' He regretted the outburst immediately, seeing how he might react as the officers were reacting if positions were reversed. 'I'm sorry, fellows, but I'm kind of worked up.'

'Then take it easy, Deely. You've been

drinking? You were drinking with Jones?'

'Yeah, that's right. No, it isn't! Look, here is the gist of the matter. I met Jones, who was a total stranger to me. He gave me to believe he was living at number twenty Willow Road.'

'But he told you a lie, huh? Well, what of it? You didn't make any bets with the guy?'

'But he isn't living there,' Butch insisted doggedly. 'At least, there's no furniture in the house. Not a scrap. Not a chair or a table or a rug, even . . .'

'The house is empty, in other words?'

'Yeah, it should be empty. I — oh, I know you guys will call me crazy, but there's a section built on to the house at the rear that shouldn't be there. I — I was curious about Jones, you see. He said his first name was Alfred. He ran into me a couple of times and gave me flowers to take to my wife.'

'Where is your wife?'

'In hospital. She's expecting a baby.'

'Go on, Deely. The house is empty, although Jones told you he was living there? He built an extension on to the house that shouldn't be there? He sent flowers to your wife in hospital? Good. We've got all that, mister. Where to now? Jones is some kind of queer bird?' he appended drily. 'How come he's queer? Queer like in — '

'I think he's a spy,' Butch blurted out heatedly. 'Yeah, I do,' he emphasized while they gaped. 'It's what I'm trying to tell you. I searched round the back of the house and it's just like ours. From the outside, that is. Inside is different. I thought I'd go and see if Jones was actually living in the house. I looked in at the front window first of all and the room was bare. I figured he might be squatting and tried the front door . . . '

'You had no right to do that, you know, Deely.'

'Yeah, I do know. Maybe I hadn't. But I tried the door and got into the house. I searched the rooms and there was nothing in any of them. Then — when I reached the kitchen — I heard these noises on the far side of the door. I opened the door and there was this room. It had an outfit of instruments or computers. They might have made up some sort of transmitting gear . . . Anyhow, they're there and I thought you ought to hear about it.'

'You aren't kidding about this, Mr Deely?' For the first time they were taking him seriously. The big fellow with the cleft chin ran his tongue over his lips and gave his leather belt a hitch up. He looked troubled, but he was ready and eager for action. His companion shut his notepad and pushed it away.

'Of course I'm not kidding. You do take me for a drunk, don't you? What do I have to say to get you to take notice?'

'Come on,' the other rapped and led the way out of the room.

In the street Butch fancied the air had turned cool. He buttoned his shirt collar and fastened the buttons of his jacket. There was a prowl car parked at the kerb, and across the road two men were standing watching. He recognized one of them as a neighbour called Bately but he couldn't say who the other man was.

The big cop told him to hitch a ride in the front. He closed Butch in on the

66

passenger side and went round to get behind the wheel. The other cop slumped on to the rear seat and emitted a heavy sigh.

'This could be our night,' he said and killed a yawn. 'It can't be so far along to twenty. You're absolutely certain this is on the level, friend? I mean, I saw a guy in court the other week. He notched three months for feeding a load of hookum to an officer. You should have seen his lower jaw hitting his boots.'

'It's on the level,' Butch said through his teeth.

They were drawing up opposite number twenty already. Butch alighted and waited for the two officers to join him. He poked a thumb at the sign nailed to a post in the yard.

'What do you call that?'

They squinted at the notice in the gloom, reading the 'For Sale' legend. Butch was walking up the drive when the officer with the cleft chin called him back.

'Come here, you.'

A hand seemed to clutch Butch by the throat, closing on his wind pipe and cutting off his breathing. A premonition had fallen on him with the weight and chill of an iceberg. Something simply had to go wrong. It just had to be one of those weird nights when you dreamed the worst nightmares, when your ulcers acted up, when you felt like walking across the ceiling to get rid of your worries and inhibitions.

He backtracked and obeyed the peremptory gesture to look at the notice on the post once more.

'Read that again.'

'Look, I don't have to take . . . ' His words trickled off and sweat made a gummy paste on his forehead. The big cop towered over him like an intimidating church spire.

'What does it say?'

'There's a sticker across the original sign. 'Sold'. What the hell! It wasn't there earlier.'

'When was earlier, chum? Last year?'

'Tonight, damn it. I'm telling you that sticker wasn't there earlier. It's freshly pasted on. I just know it is.'

The other cop was palming the red

sticker cancelling out the 'For Sale' notice. He shook his head and regarded Butch coldly.

'It's taken plenty of rain and wind. See for yourself, Deely. It's been there for quite a while.'

Butch felt the sticker and peered closely at it. His stomach gave a sickening lurch, threatening to stage an inglorious revolt. His legs trembled.

'Yeah . . . All right, then. You've got your point. But come on to the house and see what's what. You guys have got the imagination of stuffed foxes. You'll believe nothing that isn't pushed under your noses.'

'Easy, Deely. Go on and ring the doorbell some more. Don't try to enter except we tell you to. Right?'

'Look!' Butch panted, pointing to the front window. 'It's got shades on it now . . .'

'You bet it's got shades on it,' was the grim rejoinder. 'You said the window was bare. The room was bare.'

'But it was, damn it. Wait a minute!' he erupted in a paroxysm of terror. 'This isn't number twenty at all. We've mistaken the house. It's just got to be a mistake . . . '

'No mistake, Deely. Here's the numberplate. Twenty. This house doesn't look as if it's empty. I'll give you a dollar to a nickel that it's occupied.'

The cop was ringing the doorbell as he spoke. While they waited his comrade gave the door an experimental push.

'You just walked in, eh?' he sneered. 'You're one of these guys who can walk through walls?'

Butch gaped in astonishment as the door was drawn open and the bare head of Alfred Jones was thrust out.

'Yes? What can I do for you? Oh, it's police officers!' he added in some alarm. 'What do you — Butch! I didn't recognize you for a moment. Is something the matter, Butch. Your wife — '

'His wife's okay,' the big officer drawled, stabbing a sharp glare at Butch. 'Are you Mr Jones, sir?'

'Yes, my name is Jones, of course. But I'm afraid I'm completely in the dark. You see — '

70

'You won't be for long, Mr Jones. Can we come in?'

'Certainly! By all means. Dear, dear, I've never had a visit from police officers before. Forgive me if I seem a shade put about. Do come in. Come along, Butch. My, but you do look pale, Butch. You're sure that nothing has happened to your wife?'

Butch shook his head mutely. The big cop went into the hallway first but his companion held back until Butch preceded him. Alfred Jones eased past them to guide them into the living-room. Despite being put about, he seemed anxious to facilitate whatever inquiries the police officers were making.

Butch moved forward like a man in a trance, noting the beige runner on the floor of the hallway, the ornamental stand with the gaberdine raincoat and felt hat draped on it. There were two paintings on the walls: one on either side. They looked like cubist stuff which Butch could never bring himself to appreciate.

The living-room was tastefully furnished, the decor in low key. The couch and lounge chairs were Swedish style. A huge Turkish rug took up the whole centre of the floor. In one corner was a small, modest liquor cabinet. The curtains on the window were of beige, heavy silken material. Had Mona been here she could have labelled everything at once, but to Butch a chair was a chair and a drape was a drape.

Alfred Jones smiled benignly at them and indicated that they should seat themselves. For all that his legs felt robbed of every vestige of strength, Butch remained on his feet. He would not trust himself to sit in any of those chairs. By rights he should be out there in the street, running down the road at top speed and yelling warning at the pitch of his lungs. The world was going mad.

The police officers struck a solid note of sanity, and despite the threat they might offer subsequently, Butch was heartily glad to have them by him.

'Any of you gentlemen like a drink?'

'No, thank you, Mr Jones,' the cop with the cleft chin said. He cleared his throat noisily. 'Could I ask you for how long you have occupied this house, sir?'

'Indeed you can,' Jones beamed at him. 'I admit that all this is over my head. But never let it be said that I hindered the police force in the execution of their duty . . . Let me see, now. How long have I occupied this house? Oh, for two years at least, I should say. Possibly more.'

'You have the title deeds of the house in your possession, sir?'

'Certainly I have. Now let me think . . . I really did intend lodging them in my bank, but somehow or other I never got round to it. But I'm sure I can find them easily enough. Do you — '

'No, it won't be necessary, Mr Jones.' Both officers were submitting Butch to jaundiced glances. 'But why, when you bought the house so long ago, did you not remove the sign advertising the house for sale from the front yard?'

'Oh, that! Dear, dear, I never knew it would cause so much inconvenience. I'm sorry about the oversight, gentlemen. I certainly am! You don't intend to charge — But no, you don't, naturally. Creating an inconvenience is not the same thing as creating a criminal offence. You are not suggesting I'm guilty of a criminal offence, gentlemen?'

'No, we're not, Mr Jones.' They were gradually getting out of their depth and they knew it. They looked at each other.

'Could we — uh — could we see where the doorway out of your kitchen leads to, Mr Jones?'

For a moment Jones regarded them in blank amazement, then he smiled indulgently, embracing Butch in his tolerance.

'I confess I'm baffled at the request, gentlemen. But do come and look from my kitchen doorway if you must. I'm afraid there's very little to observe, apart from the weeds which I've never got around to cutting.'

They all shifted into the kitchen, Butch thrusting himself between the police officers as Alfred Jones turned the door handle and threw the door open.

All they could see in the mellow starlight was the weed-strewn yard, complete with upturned plastic bucket and discarded spade by the bushes.

5

A bird croaked from the foliage of a tree on the far side of the street. It was that kind of night: made for croaking and not for singing. Sometimes, in the early morning, you could hear a few birds singing and chirruping in the willow trees; this happened mostly in the springtime. Then, after a few weeks, the birds would disappear and Willow Road become just like any street in any other mechanical town.

It was the traffic that was doing the damage: the poisonous exhaust smokes and the clamorous noise. How could you expect any bird to vie with the noise?

'Get in, friend,' the big cop said to Butch in a restrained manner, meaning that he wished him to get into the prowl car once more.

Butch obeyed and the door was slammed on him. The rear door was slammed, also, and the cop in the back seat heaved one of his heavy sighs.

'I told you,' he informed his companion philosophically. 'It turned out to be one of those nights.'

The driver made a neat U-turn in the street and soon drew up at the front of number sixty-six.

'I'd better go into the house with you for a minute, friend,' he said to Butch. 'Hold the fort, Mike, in case something comes over the radio.'

'Will do,' his comrade agreed and nodded. He eyed the tall, strongly built figure of Butch and compared him with the height and bulk of his pal. He hoped there would be no trouble between the two. Obviously, this Deely character was a nut, but he might not have intended perpetrating real mischief. 'Make it snappy, will you, and we'll grab coffee on the way in.'

Butch opened the front door and led the way into the living-room. He was glad to see that his own house remained the same. Everything was exactly as he had left it. The furniture might be a bit scuffed and faded, but it had substance and it was real. There was no possibility of it vanishing when he turned his back on it.

He slumped down on a chair and pulled his hands across his face. Then he jumped up and hurried into the kitchen. The officer with the cleft chin followed him just as swiftly and saw Butch in the act of bringing two beer cans from the fridge.

'Would your buddy like one?' he said.

'No, he's okay. He's a coffee fiend. Drinks gallons of it during our stint.'

He took the beer can from Butch and swallowed the contents neatly. He rubbed his mouth and fingered the hard angle of his jaw.

'Now look, Deely, I don't want to be tough on you. You do understand that, don't you?'

'Yeah, I do of course.' Butch shrugged. He swallowed his beer in two thirsty gulps, flung the can at the trash bin. It missed and rolled on the tiles, letting the dregs dribble over the floor. He shrugged again, a tiredness in the shallow creases of his forehead, a look of fatalism glowing in his eyes. 'Sure, I get you. I'm a mischief maker. I phone in to the cops for the fun I get out of twisting their tails.'

'Take it easy, will you. I'm not suggesting you wanted to twist our tails. You're a truckie, Deely. I've always found truck drivers decent, respectable guys. You know?' He gave a sharp laugh. 'Let me tell you something I just remembered. Your wife's in hospital, waiting for a baby?'

'Waiting too damned long. It's overdue, and — ' He broke off there and his frown deepened. 'Say, where's the connection with Jones and the baby my wife's going to have?'

'I was getting round to it, friend. Well, I knew a fellow whose wife was expecting a baby. The way he behaved it might have been him who was expecting the baby . . . '

'Yeah, I've heard of that stuff.' Butch's grin expressed strained tolerance. 'They feel the labour pains and all. Not me, though. I've just been going about normally, and — ' He broke off once more and pursed his lips. 'Normal, huh?'

he went on bitterly. 'I'm as normal as a guy with four legs and two heads.'

'Don't be too hard on yourself,' the officer advised. 'This fellow I'm speaking of. He went through hell until the baby was born. You know what he did the night his wife had the baby? He went to the corner of the block and set a grocery store alight.'

'But I saw it,' Butch stressed wearily. 'I saw it with my own eyes . . . '

'I said to take it easy, Deely. You saw the empty house? The house that isn't empty. This bird, Jones. You haven't known him for long. Was he doing something to get on your nerves?'

'My nerves are okay.' As he spoke he was rubbing his hands on the legs of his pants, rubbing as though he wanted to make holes in the material.

'Jones hasn't been working on them? He seems a harmless, inoffensive joker, but I never judge anyone by his looks, his everyday behaviour.'

'No, of course he hasn't. But hell, he has! No, just let it ride, Officer. You don't believe me and I can't expect you to believe me. It sounds crazy and it is crazy. But the house really was empty and there was no extension built on at the back.'

'You can say that again, friend. He opened the kitchen door, didn't he? Nothing. Nothing but the back yard. So where did this strange room go to, and the instrument panels you saw? You see what I'm driving at, Delmer?'

Butch jerked at the use of his proper name. He grinned again, nodding.

'I get you. I'm sorry. Sorry I troubled you. You'll — uh — have to make out a report?'

'I guess so. But it won't go any further, I'm sure. As long as we don't have a repeat performance. Is that all right with you, Deely?' He was retreating to the door.

'That's all right with me, Officer. Thanks for everything. I'm sorry I troubled you.'

'Just forget it, Deely. Just forget it. Turn in and have a good night's sleep. Things'll look different in the morning. They always do.'

Butch accompanied him to the door

and watched him get in behind the wheel of the prowl car. The motor spun to life and the car moved off. Butch stood at the doorway until the sound of the motor faded on the night stillness.

Then he looked at his willow tree and remembered the broken limb. He should have told the cops about the broken limb of the tree as well.

'I should hell,' he growled, closing the door and heading back through to the kitchen.

The phone rang and Butch darted into the living-room and grabbed the receiver.

'Butch — I mean Delmer Deely here.'

'Mr Deely, would it be possible for you to come to the hospital at once? We think — '

'Mona!' Butch panted. 'She's having the baby? She's had the baby . . . '

'No, she hasn't, Mr Deely. There is no cause for alarm. But your wife would like you to come and see her. She's slightly upset, and you might be able to calm her down. She — '

'I'm on my way,' Butch cried hoarsely and slammed down the hand-piece.

He left the house without bothering to switch off the lights, and raced for the Olds. Driving to the end of the street, he took the corner somewhat wide and nearly tilted into a car coming from the opposite direction. After that he made a big effort to go carefully and keep his anxiety in check. The caller from the hospital had said there was no cause for alarm, but Butch knew they would say that in any event. Doctors and nurses were schooled into a professional calmness that was essential to their work.

What could have gone wrong with Mona if it was not connected with the baby? It was a query which Butch found impossible to answer. She had seemed in good health and spirits when he had seen her earlier; so what had taken place to change everything?

He was so preoccupied with thoughts of Mona and the baby that he was scarcely aware of tooling the Olds up the long hill that spiralled out of town. Luckily the road was relatively quiet and he met with no impediment or hindrance.

At length the lights of the hospital

forecourt guided him to the large sprawling building. He drove as close to the entrance as he dared without making an obstruction, sprang out and loped up the steps to the reception hall. He bypassed the desk and reached an elevator that was about to ascend. A porter was taking a small trolley load of lab bottles to an upper floor.

'Which ward do you want, mister?'

'Sixteen. The maternity wing.'

'Up she goes,' the porter grinned and closed the gate of the car. 'This your first baby, mister?'

'Yeah, it is,' Butch replied in an abstracted fashion. The elevator car appeared to be weighed down with lead.

'Well, I've got two kids myself and I know how it is. I fussed like an old hen when the first one was coming . . . This is your floor, mister. Good luck.'

'Thanks.'

Butch left the car and hurried along the corridor. An elderly woman in a matron's uniform frowned at him and halted to watch him hurtle past. He saw a nurse that he recognized and he told her he was

Delmer Deely and his wife was waiting for him.

'Go straight in, Mr Deely. But don't worry. Your wife is feeling much better. She thought it was the roses . . . '

'The roses!' Butch gulped, bypassing her and going on to the ward where his wife was located. He heaved a huge sigh of relief when he spotted Mona propped up on her pillows, with a magazine spread open that she was reading.

'Butch! I didn't intend them to fetch you back to the hospital tonight . . . Why, you're as white as a sheet. You look as if you've seen a ghost . . . '

'I was worried,' he said through his teeth. He placed a kiss on her cheek before taking the chair at the bedside. Mona's cheeks were flushed, he noticed, as though she had lately been excited over something. 'What happened, honey? What's this about the roses?' There was no sign of them on her locker or on the table in the centre of the ward where the nurses liked to put flowers eventually.

'The roses?' Mona echoed, taking his hand in her fingers. She gave a short laugh. 'Oh, it was just silly of me, I suppose, darling. You know how pregnant women get the queerest notions and phobias.'

'I know all about phobias,' he said in a steely voice. 'What was wrong with the roses? Did they upset you? But how could they? You've always liked flowers. I practically filled the house with roses on our last anniversary.'

'Easy, darling. You're all worked up. I just took this turn, you see. I couldn't understand it. The nurse couldn't understand it. She brought the doctor to see me and he decided it might be the roses. He took them away.'

'But what happened?' Butch insisted. 'How did they affect you? You had them on your locker?'

'Yes, I had. The nurse put them in a vase. She admired them. She said they were so beautiful. And they had this wonderful smell.'

'Roses always smell.' Butch straightened his untidy shirt front automatically. He must look a sight, what with his hair awry and his jacket arm soiled with the green from the tree bark. 'Did you not like the smell?'

'That's just it, Butch,' Mona said, bringing her full underlip between her teeth momentarily. 'Their fragrance was simply out of this world. When you had gone I opened them and sniffed. Do you know, Butch, it was like getting hooked on drugs. I couldn't keep myself from sniffing that wonderful perfume. After a while I began to feel ill. I — I came out in a cold sweat and the nurse grew alarmed. She brought the doctor and he gave me a thorough check over. I guess my pulse rate was up a little, but beyond that he could find nothing wrong.

'He asked me if I'd eaten something that might have disagreed with me. I couldn't think of anything. I knew it was silly, but I told him about the roses, how I had to go on smelling them once I'd got their scent in my nose.'

'What did the doctor say?' Butch demanded raggedly. 'He figured it could be the roses?'

'Yes, he said I might have developed an allergy to flowers. He suggested taking them away. He thought the whole thing was slightly amusing. He told me not to worry that I might never want to see flowers again. The allergy was probably just a temporary thing due to the pregnancy. But — but I was so upset I wanted to see you, Butch. Oh, darling, I admit I told the doctor I'd like to see you for a moment.'

'Sure, sure. I understand. If it was me I'd be the biggest cry-baby on earth. You know, I can't stand getting my finger pricked. I'm liable to faint at the sight of blood. So . . . ' He swallowed thickly and looked round the room. 'What — what did they do with the flowers, sweetie?'

'They took them to another ward, I expect. I'm sure they wouldn't dump such beautiful blossoms. But Butch, you don't think there was anything wrong with them? I mean, Mr Jones gave them to you in good faith, and — '

'Damn Jones,' he growled.

Mona laughed at the expression on his face. Yet she sobered quickly when Butch mustered a wry grin. She had never seen Butch in such a distraught state and she wondered if something else had happened between him and the stranger called Jones. Her fingers closed fiercely on his hand.

'You — you didn't see him again tonight, Butch?'

'Yeah, I — No, I didn't see him tonight, of course,' he amended swiftly. 'I was thinking about last night. It was nothing but coincidence. Jones is just a guy. A little pixilated, maybe, but harmless enough.'

'You're sure, Butch? You don't have to lie to me, you know. I've been thinking over what you said and the whole business sounds definitely odd.'

'I'd tell you a lie! Come off it, baby. Forget about that oddball, will you. You've got over your fright, or whatever it was that upset you? You're pretty certain it was the flowers?'

'What else could it have been? And they were simply flowers. Roses. What else could it have been?'

Butch wondered. He was aching to relate everything that had transpired tonight, starting at the point where he had encountered Jones once more in Wetzer's tavern. But it would be a mistake to do so. Mona would lie here and worry over it. She really would worry herself sick and perhaps endanger her condition with the baby. Later, when her confinement had come to a successful conclusion and the baby was born, he would tell her of his experiences with Jones and his house, and the police officers.

'So you're okay now,' he said with a faint smile. 'So forget it and concentrate on having that kid, huh?'

'I'm doing my best, you big lug. Oh, darling, I wish you didn't have to go home and leave me. I wish you could stay here until I'm discharged and we're riding back to Willow Road with our son.'

★ ★ ★

He had to leave Mona, of course, and he did so at midnight, kissing her fondly and assuring her that he would be back early tomorrow evening, just as soon as he put his truck away and changed his clothes.

He had made arrangements at the

depot to have any telephone calls from the hospital diverted between the hours of eight-thirty and six. All of the company's trucks were linked with radio telephone, and the signaller had promised to let him know immediately there were any developments.

On his way along the corridor to the elevator he met the pretty nurse who was in charge of Mona's ward, nights. She smiled at him and he stopped to have a word with her on the subject of the roses. He simply couldn't get those roses out of his mind and wondered if they could be part of the crazy pattern that seemed bent on enmeshing him. At first appraisal the notion had sounded ridiculous, but his experiences prior to his second visit to the hospital appeared ridiculous in retrospect. Nevertheless, Butch was convinced that his brain was sane and rational. The trouble lay not in him.

'Your wife is all right now, Mr Deely. I hope you didn't mind us getting in touch with you. Your wife was anxious and I advised the doctor to let you know.'

'I'm much obliged, Nurse, and I'm

glad that you did. Yes, my wife seems okay at the minute. She thinks it had something to do with those flowers . . . '

'The roses you brought her earlier? Yes . . . ' The nurse frowned and seemed reluctant to enlarge. 'Could I ask you if they were fresh when you bought them, Mr Deely?'

'Fresh?' Butch echoed in wonder. 'Yes, of course they were fresh. You saw them yourself, didn't you?'

'I certainly did. They looked beautiful and they had a wonderful fragrance. But I'm afraid you were gypped for all that, Mr Deely.' She blushed at his expression and went on quickly. 'You bought the roses locally, I'm sure?'

'No, wait a minute. I didn't really buy the roses myself. There is this friend, you see. Well, a neighbour rather than a friend. His name's Jones and he met me at the front of our house with the flowers. It was a nice gesture, and — But here, Nurse, what do you mean by saying I was gypped? You found something wrong with the roses?'

'You can say that again,' the girl

answered ruefully. 'No sooner had I removed them from Mrs Deely's ward than they went soft in the petals and began to wither up.'

'What!' Butch reached out to the wall to steady himself. For a moment his brain whirled in confusion. It was impossible for him to think straight.

The nurse grew concerned.

'Are you all right, Mr Deely? Please don't upset yourself about the roses. These florists are not above playing tricks, you know. They often put flowers in a fridge, and as soon as they're brought in contact with any heat they commence to wilt. All the same, I've never known flowers to fade so fast.'

'Could — could I see the roses?'

'Of course. I dropped them into the can in the office. I regretted having to do it, but what else could I do?'

Butch followed her to the small office and watched her retrieve Alfred Jones' bouquet from the trash can there. It was true what she said. Those brilliant, fragrant smelling specimens had faded into lifeless, repulsive wisps of vegetation.

6

Butch drove up through the shadows and left his car parked at the front of the garage. It would be as well to leave the Olds at the ready, he thought. He could receive another phone call from the hospital at any hour of the night, summoning him back to Mona's bedside.

He really was tired now, completely bushed. He felt sweaty and sticky all over, and he promised himself a shower as soon as he went into the house.

First, though, he walked to the driveway entrance and regarded the willow tree for a few moments. He wouldn't have been surprised to find another limb broken from the tree. Well, when things began to behave as they were doing there was no telling where the business might end.

Butch fingered a cigarette to his lips and stared along the street, first to the south and then to the north. He was

93

strongly tempted to take another stroll as far as number twenty and read that sign on the post, then circle the house to the rear and search until he came on the secret room.

On reflection, this was as silly as thinking he would return to number twenty and find the front door unlocked once more, the rooms bare and deserted once more, and no trace of the soft-spoken, blue-eyed Alfred Jones.

'Who the hell is he? Where did he spring from? How did he know so much about me? How . . . But I've asked myself these questions a hundred times. I can't see an answer. There is no answer.' The only answer that the cops or anyone else in authority would arrive at was too grim to contemplate. They would label him as a prime candidate for the cookie jar. For the time being he would have to cope on his own.

The phone began ringing as Butch walked into the living-room.

It just had to be the hospital again, he thought feverishly as he grabbed the receiver.

'Butch Deely here,' he announced tautly, forgetting to use his proper name in his anxiety. 'Is — '

'Oh, hello, Butch,' Alfred Jones greeted him in a smooth, slightly whimsical manner. 'I called twice before, Butch. After the police officers had gone, you understand. I couldn't get any response. Perhaps you have been out somewhere, Butch?'

'Yeah, I was out, as a matter of fact,' Butch hustled. 'I had to go to the hos — ' He broke off there, not wanting to describe how he had been asked to go to County Hospital to see Mona. But why did he have to relate anything to Jones? He was not obliged to keep him up to date on his movements. And yet, even as the notion crossed Butch's mind, he realized that he actually did feel compelled to give him a rundown on his behaviour.

He was fighting for breath when Jones spoke once more.

'So you went back to the hospital, Butch. I trust your dear wife was in good health when you left.'

'Yeah . . . Yes, she was.'

'I'm glad to hear it, Butch. And of course the baby has not been born yet?'

'No, it hasn't.' Butch heard a hard laugh emerge from his own lips. 'But it's bound to come any time now. Mona figured she didn't feel so well. It was the roses, she thought — '

'The roses!' Jones sounded horrified. 'Are you speaking of the roses I sent to your wife, Butch? But how could the roses have made her feel ill?'

'I — I don't know . . . ' Sweat was oozing out on Butch's brow. It trickled down his jaws in cold globules. 'Look, I'm sorry, Alfred. Please don't worry about it. It could easily have been due to something else. She could have eaten something for supper that disagreed with her.'

'Did she not like the roses?' Jones persisted. 'Did she make any comment on them?'

'Just that they smelled good. She said that once she sniffed the fragrance she just had to go on sniffing it.'

'Yes, I do understand. Your wife and I

have a little in common, Butch. Once I smell roses I've got to go on smelling them. There really is no fragrance like the fragrance of roses.'

'I agree with you, Alfred.'

'Did she get rid of them?' Jones asked suddenly.

Butch felt that he ought to relate how the roses had been taken from the ward and how they had shrivelled afterwards, looking like flowers which had been standing for a week without water. He had the oddest feeling, also, that Alfred Jones expected him to describe this very occurrence. But apart from not wishing to hurt Jones, a dim warning at the back of his brain told him to be careful.

'They — they took them to another ward. The doctor suggested that Mona's condition might have produced a temporary allergy. Anyhow, she's okay now and there's nothing to worry about.'

'I'm so glad, Butch. Now, Butch, there is something puzzling me greatly. You visited my home in company with those police officers. You had all gone before it struck me to ask what the visit was about.

The officers gave me no explanation, you understand. What did they really want, Butch?'

'Don't ask me,' Butch said defensively. He swallowed hard, but having taken the step, he continued to lie. 'They came to my house and looked around. Then they asked me to ride along to your house with them. They said they were just curious about something.'

'How distinctly odd! Well, I won't bother you further tonight, Butch. You must be tired and ready for bed. We might bump into each other again soon.'

'Sure, Alfred. Why not? Be seeing you.'

'Good-bye for now, Butch.' The line went dead.

★ ★ ★

Sound sleep was out of the question for Butch that night. He rolled and twisted restlessly, hearing himself muttering silly, disjointed phrases.

'But I didn't ask to become involved with him, Mona. It just happened. He latched himself on to me . . . I climbed up the ladder like he told me to. But the branch was already broken . . . I should have mended it, I guess. I would have mended it, only for the roses smelling that way . . . Crazy, crazy, crazy. I'm going crazy. Jones wants me to go crazy. He's sending out messages about me. Reports. He's reporting all of my movements to the police . . . Tomorrow I'll get another ladder and try again. Once I get close to those roses I'll blast them with weed-killer . . . '

Finally he could stand it no longer. He threw the covers back and switched on the bedside light. He sat on the edge of the bed and pushed his fingers through his tousled hair. Perhaps, if he was a smarter guy, he might be able to work it out satisfactorily. But he had always considered himself fairly intelligent, even if his formal education had not amounted to much. But what brand of intelligence or educated insight could show anyone the way out of this dilemma?

He wished Mona were at home with him. His wife could have helped him out of the morass he found himself in. He was convinced that the whole baffling business was centred on Alfred Jones. Who was Jones and where had he come from? Why had Jones picked on him for the purpose of . . . For the purpose of what? He was right up against the brick wall again, without a sensible lead, without any manner of clue.

Jones and his gibberish concerning the state of the world. That talk about not bringing babies into such a world.

'Babies!' Butch panted in horror. 'Oh, no! Surely he couldn't possibly prevent a woman having her baby?' Surely it was beyond the scope and machinations of anyone to interfere with a natural course of events . . .

Butch went through to the kitchen and opened the door of the fridge. He swore in frustration when he saw that he had exhausted their stock of beer. He would have to bring a pack home with him tomorrow. He slumped down on a chair and stared at the clinically clean wall of the kitchen opposite him. That was one thing he could say for Mona. She was a careful housewife. She could not bear to have dirt around. When she came home from hospital she would make him get rid of the tree branch from the back yard. She would never countenance that puddle of beer on the kitchen floor.

In an abstracted fashion Butch went to the brush and mop cubicle and brought out the mop. He felt guilty as he cleaned up the mess. Of course he should behave in the house as though Mona were here. If he were to be left alone in the house for a month he would get around to acting like a pig.

He knew this was all by the way. He was using trite detail to deflect his thoughts from the real problem. The problem consisted of Jones and the empty house he lived in that could be furnished and inhabited at a wave of the hand. He lived there and yet he did not live there. There was a chamber at the rear of the house containing a mess of sophisticated instruments, and yet there was no such chamber tagged on to the building.

At this juncture Butch realized that he would soon need help, whether it be help from the cops, the local minister, or a psychiatrist. He would simply have to take someone into his confidence. There was no other way he could think of to preserve his sanity.

'Who could he be?' he muttered, poking a cigarette to his lips and flicking his lighter aflame. He drew a lungful of smoke and blew it at the ceiling. 'But let's get one thing straight at the beginning,' he continued in a louder tone. 'You aren't going nuts. There is no history of insanity in your family. Your folks were plain, ordinary, hardworking people. Down to earth and as sane as they make them. I'm not doing anything to place a strain on my own thinking machine. All I spend my day doing is driving my truck over the country. I watch the TV and I might read the occasional book. I'm just a common or garden plain John Doe, right?

'Right,' he answered himself. 'I might be sitting here talking to myself, but it would be a hell of a lot worse if I was talking to the floor, or the wall, or the ceiling. I'm not cracked in any sense of the word. I'm sane, sane, sane. But yet I saw that notice in the front yard of number twenty. It read, 'For Sale', and I'm willing to bet my next month's salary that there was no 'Sold' sticker on the notice. Now there is a 'Sold' sticker on the board. Or is there? What might be there now if I dress and take a stroll down the street? What might number twenty look like if I go there right now and hunt around? Would Jones answer my ring on the doorbell? Would the front door be off the latch as it was earlier, and the house empty? Except for that room leading off the kitchen?'

Butch punched his cigarette into an ashtray and returned to the bedroom. He flung his robe to the bed and stripped off his pyjamas. He dressed rapidly, not thinking about what he was doing now. If he paused to reconsider he would undoubtedly take cold feet and stay where he was.

A few minutes later he left the house quietly, making sure he had his key in his pocket before drawing the door shut. The sight of his car was a solid and comforting reminder that there were solid and comforting familiar objects within the reach of an outstretched hand.

The street was still; the lamps at each end of the road glowed like warm, reassuring beacons. He commenced walking, moving in nervous, jerky motion at first, but then schooling his gait to the semblance of a contained, leisurely stroll.

He encountered no one on the way, saw no car, no person, no stray mutt on a scavening expedition. His heart began pounding as he neared number twenty. From this distance he could spot the notice in the front yard. He should have brought his flashlight with him, but he could see well enough when he was closer to the sign.

The driveway leading up to number twenty was deserted. No car was parked near the garage, although Jones could have run the Ford into the garage for the night. The night? The time was getting on to three in the morning. The stars had started to pale and in an hour or so false dawn would be smudging the eastern heavens.

Butch froze at the end of the driveway, feeling that, by now familiar, prickling sensation at the nape of his neck. His legs threatened to betray him at the last moment. He willed them to carry him across the yard to where the sign was located. He stood directly in front of it and read the notice.

'For Sale.' Nothing else. No sticker cancelling the agent's advertisement.

Butch closed his eyes for a moment, then opened them and looked at the sign once more. He wished those cops could be with him at this minute. He envied them their stark, realistic outlook, their ability to be cynical in the face of almost every problem they were called on to deal with.

But the query remained: what had become of the sticker that had borne evidence to the way the sunlight had faded it, the way the wind and rain had fretted the edges?

Moving like a man sleep-walking, Butch continued to the front window of the house and halted there with the blood turning to ice water in his veins. There were no drapes on the window, no shades of any description. He put his sweaty face to the glass and cupped his hands about his eyes as he had done earlier. All that he saw beyond the scummy glass was a bare room.

Butch could have easily been forgiven had his nerve broken into irreplaceable shreds. It was enough to test the nerve and sanity of a stronger man. He was aware of that warning clamour at the back of his brain.

'Get out of here at once. Don't hesitate for another moment. Get back home immediately and call the cops.'

Yet, some stronger, more impelling force held him rooted to the spot. No, he would not run. There was too much at stake for him to retreat from here. There was Mona in hospital, waiting, depending on him. There was the unborn baby to be considered. He had too many responsibilities weighing on him to dispose of them lightly. Whatever Jones was up to, he was fit enough and able enough to play him at his own game.

Perhaps this marked the point where sanity really did wilt under the burden it was being asked to bear. Recklessness was closely allied to the rejection of reason and logic. The situation had no reason, and neither had it logic. Recklessness could be interpreted at times as sheer calculated boldness in the face of an encompassing problem, but it would have required the skill of a professional to define dividing or border lines. Butch Deely was no practised psychologist.

He moved to the front door of the house and gave it a gentle push. The door eased inwards, letting Butch see a dark, empty hallway that reeked of stale air. He took one tentative step beyond the doorway, another. He halted and balled his fists instinctively.

'Mr Jones . . . Alfred . . . Are you there?'

His voice came back like the obliging vibrations from an echo chamber. This house was empty. There was nothing here to offer obstruction or danger. Nothing but that secret chamber at the rear . . .

Would it still be there when he reached the kitchen and opened the door that should give on to the back yard, the weeds the clutter of bushes, the plastic bucket and the spade?

Butch went forward.

By the time he reached the kitchen his breathing was rapid and shallow. He could imagine all sorts of frightening possibilities. Alfred Jones would return to the house from wherever he had gone to. He would crack his fingers and the house would once again be fully furnished. He would stand there, laughing at Butch, and tell him he was due to be locked up in a mental asylum. Or those cops would come back to have another look at number twenty Willow Road. They would find the door open and walk in. They would seize the intruder and take him to headquarters on a charge of breaking and entering.

In Butch's estimation, it would be fine if the police officers did arrive and join him right now. They would see for themselves that the house was now empty and he had been telling the truth.

But the police officers would not come. Neither would Alfred Jones put in an appearance. There was a definite pattern here, even if it was an impossibly fantastic one.

He held his breath and listened for the tell-tale clickings and tappings on the other side of the kitchen door. There was a shrill shriek that sent a shaft of terror racing up his spine. The noise was followed by a mighty scuffling. Then he heard a cat mewing loudly and he touched his dry lips with the tip of his tongue.

Nothing else. The cats seemed to have gone; there was silence once more. No tappings came from the far side of the kitchen door. He moved towards the door and gripped the handle firmly. He opened the door and heaved it outwards; as he did so he wondered, incongruously, why this door should open outwards at all. But it did and there was nothing on the other side but the shadowed yard overhung by a sky speckled with wan stars.

The pent-up breath ran from Butch's lungs in a shuddering sigh. Perhaps this was the end of the matter, he thought hopefully. He had stumbled on Jones' secret and he had taken steps to have the secret chamber removed.

Ridiculous? Of course it was ridiculous. The whole concept featuring the stranger was ridiculous in the extreme, fantastic as the most outrageous fantasy could be. But it could have come to an end, nevertheless. Alfred Jones realized that he wasn't dealing with a soft mark when he was dealing with Butch Deely. He had decided to pull in his horns and . . . Horns! Yes, there was an apt thought and no mistake. But he wasn't here and that was what mattered. The furnishings had gone and the secret room had gone. Would a state of normality be introduced now and allowed to prevail?

Butch shrugged his heavy shoulders, wearying of these speculations. He felt depleted at this juncture, both physically and mentally; even spiritually depleted. He could not bring himself to retrace his steps through this haunted house. What else could it be called but haunted?

He stepped out to the back yard and pushed the door shut behind him. The air had cooled considerably and he was glad of the breeze that touched his cheeks. He wiped the cold sweat from his brow and jaws. He walked on to the corner of the house where the rear end of the garage jutted out and halted, jerking his head suddenly to look up at the star-strewn sky. It had seemed to him that one of those stars had flared into blinding brightness. But the sky appeared normal and it must have been his imagination. About now his imagination was capable of conjuring up anything.

The star flared afresh and he watched it, spellbound. A radiation stabbed earthwards and Butch was forced to close his eyes and turn his head away. After a moment he risked looking upwards again. The star had disappeared, or its light had dwindled to the mellow glow of its neighbours.

Butch lumbered past the side of the garage and soon reached the street. He walked rapidly towards his own house, not looking backwards, not looking upwards. He had the eerie sensation that Alfred Jones was watching him all the way.

7

At eight o'clock Butch rolled off the couch where he had lain down on his return from Jones' house. For about four hours he had slept the sleep of the utterly exhausted. It had been a deep, dreamless sleep, and it seemed to have repaired a lot of the nervous damage he had suffered.

His first thought on opening his eyes was for Mona, and he went over to pick up the telephone, slumping down on a chair with the instrument in his lap. He yawned and rubbed his eyes, and when his eyes could focus well enough he dialled the County Hospital number with an unsteady forefinger.

'Sorry to trouble you so early in the morning,' he said to the thin-voiced woman who took the call. 'I'm Delmer Deely and I'm inquiring about Mrs Deely in maternity . . . '

'Hold on, please,' the voice said before he had time to enlarge. Then, about a minute later, 'Mrs Deely is comfortable. She had a good night. She's still asleep, as a matter of fact.'

'Good,' Butch said. 'Good.' Then the anxiety came back to gnaw at him. 'There's no sign of — I mean, the baby hasn't been born yet?'

'No, Mr Deely. We expect your wife to go into labour today. But of course there is no guarantee, as you'll appreciate. It's just one of those things.'

'I understand. Thank you. I'll call back later if I may. I guess I'm making a nuisance out of myself,' he added with a weak chuckle.

'On the contrary, Mr Deely. We welcome all enquiries concerning patients.'

'Of course. Thank you. Good-bye.'

He sighed and put the instrument back on to its stand.

Holy smoke, it was after eight, and he'd intended being on the road to Ferndale with his truck at eight-thirty this morning. It was Wednesday today, and his first run of the day every Wednesday was to Ferndale, a hundred-odd miles upstate.

He didn't feel much like going to work

at all, he reflected, making coffee in the kitchen. And if it wasn't Wednesday he'd ring in to Cowan, the manager, and tell him he was sick.

He was sick, too. Sick to the teeth with worry and foreboding. He had the feeling that he could not go on for much longer with things as they were. Something was bound to give. He was only flesh and blood, after all, and there was a limit to what he could take. What he needed was advice from someone — maybe a doctor's advice. But how would any doctor react to the tale that he unfolded? He would be treated as someone headed for a breakdown. He would be told to take it easy, to forget his work and forget his worry over Mona and the baby.

A medico would point to this as the seat of the trouble. He could see Doc Woodford smiling gently at him across the frames of his horn-rimmed glasses. He could almost hear Woodford telling him that there was nothing wrong with his mind. Everyone imagined occasionally that they saw things which did not actually exist. There was a name for that, too — hallucinations. So long as he did not allow himself to become obsessed with them he would be okay.

It was Woodford or a psychiatrist. Unless he thought he could win the battle by himself. But Butch Deely would rather submit himself to any amount of strain in preference to presenting himself to a psychiatrist for examination and treatment. He was convinced he was healthy and sane. But some plot was afoot to unbalance him.

At eight forty-five he left the house and drove his car out to the street. It was a clean, bright morning with a blue sky overhead that promised a warm day. He thought of last night and that star and shuddered. He must forget it for the moment. He must grit his teeth and hold on somehow. He must pin his hopes to the belief that everything would turn out all right eventually.

If only he could forget that such a man as Alfred Jones existed.

Did Jones actually exist?

Butch was about to drive off when a voice hailed him and he turned his head, at the same time removing his foot from the accelerator. Andy Midgley was hurrying from the front of his house to speak to him. The alarm that had begun coiling in Butch subsided.

'I won't keep you a minute, Deely.' Midgley had the habit of using second names, but he did it in such a manner that no offence could be taken. When Andy Midgley greeted you he made you feel as if you were an old pal and he could say what he liked to you. 'I really don't know how you can forgive us,' he went on, rubbing the back of his thick neck. 'About your wife, I mean, Deely. But I figured it would have been all over by now. She's still in the hospital, isn't she?'

'Yeah, she is, Andy.' Butch glanced at his wristwatch and gave the gas pedal a tap with his toe. 'But she's doing okay and she should be getting home any time.'

'Say, that's swell. I'm pleased to hear it. Don't forget to give her our regards. You're kind of late this morning.'

'I know. I'll have to push. I — '

Butch's voice trickled off as he saw

someone else on the street, far down as yet, but coming in this direction. Andy Midgley wondered at the way Butch paled, and he switched his gaze, seeing the man in the raincoat and felt hat, also.

'Who is that guy, Deely? I've seen him go past here a couple of times. He's new to the district, isn't he?'

'So you don't know him?' Butch asked in a tone that vibrated slightly. 'He's supposed to be living in the house Mrs Consby left. You know, number twenty.'

'Oh yeah, I do remember Mrs Consby. Quaint old dame, she was. No, that guy is a stranger to me. What do they call him?'

'Jones. Alfred Jones.' Butch knew he should be on the move, but it would be worth losing another few minutes if he could learn anything fresh on the newcomer. Jones had come to a halt and was staring up at the branches of one of the trees in the street. Butch guessed that a few birds were roosting there and he was watching their antics. He suddenly recalled the damage suffered by his own willow tree. 'I thought number twenty was empty,' he remarked tentatively, pulling his eyes back to Midgley.

'Yeah, so did I. It's been lying idle for a long time. Last time I looked in there, the agent's notice was in the yard.'

'It's still there,' Butch said casually.

'What! Is Jones off his noodle? Well, I won't keep you, Deely. Oh, say, I noticed you lost a branch from the tree fronting your house. What happened to it?'

'I don't know, Andy. It was broken when I got home yesterday. You didn't see any of the kids around?'

Midgley shook his head. He was watching Alfred Jones again. A cat had come from somewhere and Jones was stooped over the animal, rubbing it while it arched its back and pushed itself against his ankles. Butch could imagine the cat purring like ninety.

'I can't stand damned cats,' Midgley said feelingly. 'No, I didn't see any kids near your tree, Deely. All the kids in this neighbourhood are growing up fast. You remember how we used to play with hoops and marbles and things? Kids have quit playing those games, have you noticed? They spend their time squatting on their tails in the drugstores. Necking with the girls before they've outgrown their pimples and freckles. Times have changed, Deely. You know, speaking about kids, I was just saying to my wife the other day that they're getting scarcer every year. Babies, I mean.' He laughed. 'We were talking about your wife and her forthcoming baby. I happened to say that not many folks on this street had babies. My wife reminded me that there hasn't been a baby born to a couple on this street for two or three years. I guess we're finally getting the message, Deely, eh? When your kid comes along you'll be kind of unique.'

He laughed again, but Butch could see nothing funny in the remark. He waved to Midgley and sent the Olds forward. He was glad that he normally left the street by the north end, so that Alfred Jones would not imagine he was deliberately ducking him. He glanced in his rear-view mirror and his jaw fell. There was no sign of Alfred Jones now. He could see the cat right enough. It was rubbing itself against the bole of the tree where the birds must have been singing, but of the blue-eyed, bespectacled stranger there was no trace.

Butch had something else to chew on as he drove to the truck depot. No babies had been born to any couple on Willow Road for the last two or three years. Yes, he reflected with a surge of excitement pulling at his groin, it was perfectly true. There were no babies as such on Willow Road at present. Oh, there were dozens of kids, of course, but as Midgley had observed to him, they were moving towards adulthood and they didn't hang around the street as they used to.

Was there any connection between that and . . . But no, of course there wasn't. His imagination might invest Alfred Jones with any number of queer, unnerving talents, but certainly the stranger could not exert any manner of control over the birth-rate.

' . . . You know, Butch, I often wonder if it's right to bring children into such a world . . . I'm trying to say this, not enough time and energy are devoted by the people of the world to the task of making it perfect . . . '

Pete Rawlins had the motor of the truck running by the time Butch finally reached the depot and left his car on the parking space reserved for employees. Stout, balding Sam Cowan saw his arrival through the office window and hurried out to meet him. Cowan prided himself on the customary smooth running of operations, and when a snag cropped up to upset things he wasn't slow to take it out on the culprit. He knew, however, that Butch's wife was in hospital expecting their first baby, and being a father of three children himself he was prepared to make some small allowances.

'You're late, Butch,' he said in his high-pitched, reedy voice. 'I'd decided to wait until nine-fifteen before calling in a rest-day man. Is everything okay?' he added with a perceptible softening of tone. 'Your wife hasn't given birth yet?'

'No, she hasn't, Mr Cowan. Yeah, everything's okay as far as it goes. I'm sorry I'm late.'

'Forget it,' Cowan said, reverting to his

usual brusque delivery. 'I told Pete there's a container to be picked up at Stettner's on Commercial Avenue. Leave it off at their branch in Ferndale. The other stuff's loaded and Pete has got the invoices.'

'Okay, Mr Cowan.' He cut out to join Rawlins in the cab of the big glistening truck, then halted and spoke across his shoulder. 'You'll contact me if some news comes through from the hospital?'

'Of course, Butch. Sally will do exactly that.'

Pete moved over and Butch climbed on to his seat. Pete said, 'Hi, pal. Figured you were going to spend the day in bed. They fixed that spring we reported last night. Joe says he replaced it with a good one. What's new, Butch?'

'Nothing much, Pete.' Butch tooled the large vehicle out of the yard and swung left to gain the centre of Caldwell. He saw a dusty Volkswagen move off from the kerb behind him, but he paid no attention to the car or the driver.

'The kid hasn't shown himself yet, huh?' the middle-aged Rawlins said sympathetically. 'Well, quit worrying. In a month or so you'll think back and wonder why you lost a wink of sleep. When he's pulling the house apart round your ears that'll be the time to worry. You know?'

'Sure, Pete. I'm not worrying. Everything's going to be okay.'

He negotiated the heavy morning traffic stream and drew up alongside Stettner's hardware store. Rawlins unlocked the truck doors and the container was taken on. Glancing in his wing mirror before pulling out, Butch noticed a dusty grey Volkswagen with a lean, dark-featured man at the wheel. On this occasion the presence of the car registered.

'Who's that?' he said to Rawlins, jerking his thumb. 'Sam isn't doing one of his spot checks on us?'

'The beetle? Naw, I wouldn't say so. Just some joker who likes watching trucks. You know, it's how I decided to take up truck driving, Butch. I used to watch them go by the front door when I was a button. The buses, too. I couldn't make up my mind whether to be a bus driver or a truck driver.'

'Oh, yeah? I always wanted to be a train

driver. You must have had a twist in your childish ambitions, Pete. Every kid worth his salt wants to be a train driver.'

'Not nowadays, pal,' Pete said with a chuckle. 'My Jody figures he's going to be an astronaut when he grows up. Oh, I don't know. Maybe it's got something to do with progress. Me, I took to truck driving like a fish taking to water. Then I got this trick shoulder in Korea and here I am, little better than a flunkey for the real truck drivers. Still, it was nice of old Sam taking me back and giving me a job. What could a joe with a trick shoulder do to earn a living, I ask you?'

'Please, Pete, don't make me weep so early in the day. You've seen too many John Wayne pictures in your time. Everybody can't be a hero with a charmed life.'

On the main highway to Ferndale, Butch kept the big truck rolling along at seventy. It really was a dream to handle, and the motor purred throatily like a contented cat. In this setting it was difficult to think of last night's events as anything but the products of an outsize nightmare. He tried to forget Alfred Jones and concentrate exclusively on Mona lying in that hospital bed, brave and patient, and bearing the brunt of the burden. But, inevitably, visions of that house on Willow Road intruded, and when they did Butch Deely's brow became layered with a cold sweat.

On reaching Ferndale, they distributed their load and went on to the branch depot to pick up the usual consignment of empty containers. It was their custom to leave the truck at the depot and have a meal at a nearby café. It was called a grill-room.

During the meal Pete Rawlins went through the sports section of a newspaper he had brought with him from Caldwell. Sometimes he played the horses, as did Butch on a modest scale. But since Mona had gone into hospital Butch had lost interest in the racing. He sipped his coffee and smoked a cigarette and gazed idly at the section of the Caldwell Courier facing him. A minor headline half-way down the page caught his attention.

'DRAMATIC FALL IN CITY BIRTH-RATE.'

'Here, give me that page,' he said to Rawlins and drew it across the table with unsteady fingers. Pete paid no heed as he read the report avidly. It seemed that a recent census produced by the hospitals' authority had shown a distinct falling off in the number of babies born in Caldwell during the past two years. 'Making a comparison with the birth-rate in the state in general, it emerges that Caldwell is way, way behind in the baby stakes. Naturally, the authorities see no cause for alarm, and it might be said that Caldwell is blazing a responsible trail. All the same, studies are in progress to determine the exact reason for the dearth of babies . . . '

At that moment Pete Rawlins laid his newspaper aside to search his pockets for cigarettes. His good-humoured gaze lifted to Butch's face and froze there.

'Say, what's the matter, Butch? Did you see something in the news to upset you?'

'No,' Butch mumbled, mustering a tortured smile to his features. 'Of course not . . . '

'Here, let me have a gander.' He took the remaining sheets of the Courier from

Butch's fingers and scanned the page he had been reading.

'Hell, Pete, didn't I tell you — '

'All right, all right. Don't go up in smoke. You've been behaving queer for the last couple of days, pal. Why don't you spit it out? You know, get it off your chest . . . Oh, I get it. This thing about the falling birth-rate in town. So what? Everybody knows there's far too many kids being born. Why else would they be so keen to put this family planning gag over to — '

'Shut up, Pete,' Butch snarled at him. As soon as he had spoken he regretted the outburst. Rawlins took a long breath and eyed his buddy curiously. He shrugged and grinned.

'I'm sorry, Butch. Me and my big mouth. Just forget it, will you?'

'Yeah, I will. I'm sorry, Pete,' Butch appended contritely. 'But this damned waiting is getting on my nerves.'

'Don't I know it, boy! You don't have to tell me anything about being an expectant father. I've had it from here to there.'

Rawlins laughed uneasily and glanced

at his wristwatch.

'Well, if we pull out now we'll have made up lost time. How about it, Butch?' He was somewhat red in the face with embarrassment. He really did think Butch was taking it too far. The way he was behaving there was something special about his fathering a baby. He fingered his cigarette to his lips and lighted it. He rose and Butch came to his feet also. There was a whiteness about Butch's mouth that worried Rawlins.

'I'm sorry, Pete.'

'Let it ride, pal.'

Pete led the way out of the café to the street. Butch was going past the booth nearest the street door when he saw the man sitting alone with a coffee cup and empty plate in front of him. His stomach knotted. He was certain that this lean, dark-featured character was the person who had been driving the Volkswagen. But who was he, and why the hell was he following him around?

The man looked up and their eyes met. The stranger gave Butch a cool nod and lowered his gaze to the table. Butch fought with an urge to challenge him; he conquered it and went after Pete Rawlins to the sunshine.

For the remainder of that day Butch kept looking in his mirrors for sign of the dusty grey Volkswagen and the thin man who had obviously been following him. He failed to spot any trace of the car again, but he was certain, nevertheless, that he was being kept under surveillance. And if the tail hadn't been put on by Sam Cowan, the depot manager, who, then, was responsible?

★   ★   ★

Butch was glad when it was time to drive the truck into the depot yard at the end of the day. He left Pete Rawlins with a gruff so-long and hurried to his Olds on the parking area. His mood was such that it dictated he should make a slight round-about so as to enter Willow Road by the south end and drive past number twenty.

He slowed on his approach to the front yard of the house and noted with a shock how the 'For Sale' notice had been removed from the weeds. Also, Alfred Jones' Ford was parked opposite the garage doors.

Butch continued to his own driveway and eased on to the asphalt. As he alighted he heard another car coming to a halt at the kerb. He jerked about and mouthed a hard curse on recognizing the grey Volkswagen with the lean man at the wheel.

8

The driver of the Volkswagen sat there for a moment, looking round him, then he alighted in a leisurely sort of way, giving the impression that he never hurried and seldom allowed anything to knock him off his stride.

He gave the slack-jawed Butch a faint smile and said hello. He added in a measured tone that had enough confidence in it to make Butch wonder, 'Your name's Deely?'

'You ought to know that by now,' Butch said roughly. He saw how the stranger could easily grasp the initiative. He gave you the feeling that he was accustomed to grasping the initiative. But there was nothing overbearing or heavy-handed about him — just this quiet aura hinting at strength and resilience. He seemed like a person who could be really nice to you or really nasty to you.

He poked a cigarette to his narrow lips and chuckled.

'I'm sorry. I didn't intend to rattle you, Deely. What is your first name — David? Delmer?'

'Folks call me Butch.' Butch thought he had him weighed up by then. He was either a cop or a snooper employed by the trucking company. He turned his head and saw old Hornbeck squinting curiously across his hedge. He lifted a hand in salute and Butch acknowledged it. 'I guess you'd better come in if you want to talk,' he told the stranger. 'That's the general idea, isn't it?'

'If it isn't putting you to too much bother, Butch.'

So far he had not disclosed his own name or the nature of his business. Butch shrugged and went on to open the front door. He spoke over his shoulder.

'I'm afraid it'll have to be snappy. My wife's in hospital, you see. As soon as I get home from work I change and drive to the hospital to see my wife.'

'That's the County, isn't it?'

Butch said it was. He flung the door

wide open and led the way towards the living-room.

'I won't delay you, Butch,' the thin man said behind him. 'I'll tell you what. I'll talk while you shave and dress, or whatever it is you do. You make a meal?'

'Just coffee.' Butch decided he could take on with the stranger easily enough. His nature invited friendship. But it might just be a front. These guys were chosen for their jobs with the greatest care. Psychological charts and birthday signs and whatnot were used to select the right candidate. Butch threw his working jacket at a chair. He had a good look at the dark-featured man and indicated another chair.

'No, I won't sit down. Look, don't let me put you out, Butch. Simply carry on as if I'm not here. I know the sort of heavy day that you fellows put in.'

'How did you discover that?' Butch asked with irony. He discarded his necktie and pulled his shirt off. 'Would you care for a drink of java yourself?'

'Yeah, I would. Look, show me where the kitchen is and I'll make like a three-star chef. Oh, by the way, Butch, my name is Hartman. Frank Hartman.'

'Hi, Frank,' Butch said with a sour grin. He was almost past worrying about people and their motives. If Hartman was a company snoop then let him snoop. So what? If he was a cop wanting to reopen the incident of the empty house that wasn't really empty at all, then let him go to it. So what? Just then Butch was thinking of Mona and wondering how he would find her when he arrived at the hospital this evening. He pointed towards the kitchen. 'In there.'

'Right. I'll fix the coffee, Butch.' He plucked his cigarette from his lips and mashed it in a tray. He gave Butch a slightly whimsical grin. 'You're not worried about me following you around today?'

'Of course I'm not.' Butch was starting for the bathroom. 'I'm so popular I get fan-mail. Today was one of the slack days for my admirers. Usually five or six guys follow me around in my truck.' He stopped and wheeled to face Hartman, and for a moment the burden he carried weighed as heavy as lead. 'What's on your mind, mister?' he asked hollowly. 'You a company man?'

'I'm a cop, Butch,' Hartman confessed. He had small dark eyes that went over Butch swiftly and carefully, missing nothing on their journey. He brought a wallet from his hip pocket and flipped it open, watching the surprise register on the trucker's rugged features.

'Federal bureau of investigation?' Butch gulped, aware of being jolted out of his indifference. 'So I'm that important? I just don't get it.'

'Maybe you do,' Hartman said gently, closing the wallet and replacing it in his pocket. 'Maybe you don't. I'm not here of my own accord, Butch. We're all workers in this world. Some of us drive trucks. Some of us get ambitious and go to work for Uncle Sam. Uncle Sam isn't such a bad guy, Butch. You agree?'

'Yeah, I do. But the F.B.I.? It has to do with the cops being here?'

'It has to do with the cops being here,' Hartman agreed. He thought of something and fingered his rather sharp chin.

'I'll tell you what, Butch. I'll grab a cup of coffee some place else. I won't hold you back. What time do you usually return home from the hospital?'

'Nine. Nine-thirty. Sometimes later.'

'How would it do if I came visiting again at ten? And you don't have to put the news around. I'm just an old pal from bygone days, huh?'

'Yes, all right,' Butch said with his eyes shining. 'So those fellows didn't really figure I was crazy?'

'Let's say I don't figure you're crazy. That should be enough to get along with.' He straightened his hat and moved towards the room door. 'Ten o'clock?'

'Yeah, yeah . . . I'll be here at ten o'clock. But I've got to warn you it's a nutty tale, friend.'

'I'm used to nutty tales,' Hartman smiled. 'You care to hear how many Ufo stories I've investigated?'

'Ufo?' Butch echoed. He laughed shakily. 'Not like in unidentified flying objects?'

'Just like that, Butch. But I'm not a nut either, you must understand. I've got several degrees to prove I'm quite a head-piece. This happens to be my line. The offbeat, that is. What I heard about you intrigues me. Okay till ten?'

'Sure, Mr Hartman.'

'Call me Frank, Butch. 'Bye for now. Hope your wife is in good form when you see her.'

He left the house on that note and Butch went on to have his shower before making coffee.

★　★　★

Alfred Jones was waiting for him at the end of the driveway.

Butch failed to see him until the last moment, and he stabbed for the brake pedal, muttering an oath and bringing the Olds to a halt beside the stranger. If Jones noticed the way Butch's face pulled into a taut mask at sight of him he gave no indication that he did. He smiled widely at Butch and proffered a small, colourfully wrapped parcel.

'You're on your way to the hospital to see your good lady, I gather, Butch?'

'Yes, I am.' Butch attempted to school his features to a neutral expression. 'What's this, Alfred? Not another present for Mona? But it's too much, Alfred.'

'Of course it isn't.' He seemed hurt at Butch's reluctance to accept the parcel and Butch took it from him, placing it by his side on the seat. 'Candies, Butch. Most women like candies. I'm sure that Mrs Deely will enjoy them.' He looked wistful now as he said that. He had discarded his raincoat and hat, and was wearing a neat grey suit which made him appear very spruce and immaculate. 'You must allow me to indulge myself, Butch. After all, I have so few friends. True friends,' he added with a trace of sadness in his voice. 'Without friends you are inclined to get lonely. But you must know what it's like to be lonely, Butch.'

'Yeah, I do, Alfred.' Butch grinned sheepishly, relenting, Jones seemed to have the knack of producing the effects he sought after. He wondered if Jones knew of the visit from Frank Hartman earlier. He suspected that he made it his business to keep abreast with the most trivial

138

events on the street. 'Well, thanks for the candies,' he said, wanting to get on the move. 'I'm sure Mona will be delighted with them.'

'I sincerely hope so, Butch. Give your wife my best regards. Oh, by the way, I was going to ask you to drop in on me some evening when it's convenient. I should enjoy another chat with you, Butch. You know' — his blue eyes twinkled behind the lenses of his spectacles — 'we might continue our discourse on social philosophy to some degree. I'm certain we have a lot in common. Does the idea appeal to you?'

It appealed to Butch just then the way jumping from the roof of a block of high-rise apartments would appeal to him. Nevertheless, he grinned and inclined his head.

'Say, that's a real good idea, Alfred. I might take you up on it. Thanks.'

'So-long for the present, Butch.'

Butch sweated slightly as he tooled the Olds to the end of the street, squinting in his rear-view mirror as he felt impelled to do, and experiencing only the mildest surprise at the absence of Jones on the street.

'So what?' he muttered bitterly, taking the corner and cuffing the cold moisture from his brow. 'He comes and he goes. Where he come from and where he goes, nobody knows.'

He shot a glance at the neatly wrapped parcel on the seat beside him and shuddered. A box of candies for Mona tonight. A bouquet of roses for Mona last night. What the hell was he trying to do to Mona — make her really sick so that she would lose the baby?

Still, it was too late for Jones to bring any manner of sinister influence to bear on his wife in the interests of preventing the birth of yet another child. Jones might be smart up to a point, but whatever grades he had passed in social philosophy, he had muffed his biology test with a vengeance.

Butch endeavoured to push Alfred Jones from his mind. He would concentrate on Frank Hartman instead. He was rather looking forward to a session with the F.B.I. man tonight when he got home.

Hartman might be the remedy he needed so badly. He looked cool enough and thoroughly intelligent, and it was a cinch he would not give him the horse laugh when he heard all about that queer house with the invisible chamber at the rear.

'Don't bank on it, buddy,' he mused thinly. 'Unidentified flying objects might be a field that Hartman is familiar with, but I'm willing to bet anything he's never heard of anyone like little old Alfred Jones.'

★ ★ ★

Butch left the box of candies in the car on reaching the hospital. He was not going to put Mona at risk again tonight. He had a vague notion of handing the candies to Hartman and having him run an analysis on them. Hartman could do it easily enough, and the results might boomerang on Jones in a way he had never suspected.

Mona was sitting up in bed, smiling cheerfully, when he walked into the ward, and a glance was enough to tell him that the baby was still holding back. She had her long, silken hair brushed becomingly, and when he kissed her cheek he marvelled at the sheer softness of her skin.

'For pete's sake, honey, hurry up and get this over,' he growled throatily. 'Being without you for so long is like being locked up in solitary confinement.'

Mona laughed as he sat down on the bedside chair. She automatically lifted his hand and began playing with his fingers.

'It mightn't last for much longer, Butch. I had a lot of pain earlier today. The doctor has been with me twice, and he's sure I'll go into labour any time.'

'Swell, baby. That's just swell. You didn't have any more of that sickness. You know, the feeling you had when you kept smelling the roses?'

'Not a thing, darling. I'm feeling grand. I know I'm fighting fit. Well, as fighting fit as can be expected in the circumstances. But Butch,' she added in a different tone, 'you didn't bring me any, did you? I was so hoping you would. I was making small bets with myself before you arrived. I got this craving, and I was sure you would know all about it.'

'Know all about what?' he demanded shakily. 'You've got a craving for something? A craving for what, Mona?'

'Candies,' she announced with a giggle. 'Isn't it a scream? Me wanting candies. You know how I steer clear of candies to keep my weight down. But today I would have given anything for a feast of them. Just like a pregnant woman, huh?'

'Yeah,' Butch said hoarsely, evading her eyes for an instant. He gave a rough laugh. 'Look, you'll never believe what I'm going to tell you. That guy Jones — remember him? Well, he was waiting for me at the end of the driveway. And what did he hand me as a gift for my darling wife?'

'A box of candies? But surely not, Butch! How could Mr Jones be more aware of my whims and needs than you are? But where are they? Don't tell me. You forgot them. You left the box in the car down below?'

'I did,' Butch said, patting at his brow. 'But I didn't forget them, honey. I just remembered that you went off sweet stuff, and figured I was doing you a favour.'

'Okay then,' Mona said with a mischievous smile. 'You go right downstairs and fetch Mr Jones' present . . . Butch,' she added while her fingers closed on his hand. 'You — you don't think there is anything wrong with the candies?'

'Of course I don't.' He released his hand and stood up. 'You sit tight and I'll bring the box up, baby.'

He left her abruptly, endeavouring to look cheerful and confident as he walked out of the ward. When he reached the elevator the car was between floors and he had to wait a few minutes until it was available. He hurried on out to the cool night air and brought a huge gulp of it to his lungs. Just then he had the sensation of being manipulated. He was not a free agent any longer, but was no more independent than a puppet on a string. Somebody was standing back there, watching him, laughing at him, challenging him to get off the hook if he could.

He walked over to the Olds, thinking murderously of Alfred Jones. A further example of plain coincidence? Not on your life, it wasn't. Some kind of dark plot was in the making and he was one of the characters in the plot, albeit a reluctant actor. But why, why, why? What was the reason behind it? Was there really some hidden link holding each segment of events together?

He hoped he was not going crazy. He just hoped that someone was not bent on driving him crazy. For the first time it came to him that there actually could be circumstances in which a sane and down-to-earth person might contemplate murder.

Butch fumbled for his keys and unlocked the driving side door of the Olds. His fingers were closing on the wrapping of the box of candies when he had an inspiration. A mile or so along the road to the north of the hospital location there was a gas station and a small general store. He could quite easily get a replacement for the box of candies there; a substitute, he reflected with a grim smile at his lips.

No sooner had the idea crossed his

mind than he slid in behind the wheel and slammed the door. He accelerated smartly to the entrance and turned to the right. He drove fast, not wanting to be away from Mona for long. A short time later he parked opposite the store and regarded the brightly lit show window. Yes, there was a large box of candies that would satisfy his wife's yen for sweetmeats.

He went in and bought the candies, and when the clerk reached for a sheet of plain wrapping paper he asked if they had no coloured presentation paper.

'Of course, sir. Any particular colour?'

'Have you got pink?' he said on impulse. 'It's for my wife in the hospital, you understand, and — '

'This will look quite gay, sir. I hope your wife is keeping well. But she must be on the mend if she's able to eat candies.'

'We're going to have a baby,' Butch confided for no particular reason that he could account for.

'Really? Congratulations, sir. Then my very best wishes go along with this.'

'Thanks.' He grabbed the parcel and

paid. He felt slightly easier in his mind as he hurried to the Olds and retraced his way to the hospital. By now Mona would be having kittens, never mind a baby, he thought wryly.

He parked and hastened back into the foyer. The elevator was about to go up and he pushed himself inside with five other visitors. When it reached his floor he dashed out and went on to Mona's ward.

'Hi again, baby,' he grinned, giving her the parcel, noticing the concern that was mirrored in her eyes. 'Sorry it took me so long. But a guy wanted to get out of the parking area and I had to shift the car.'

'Yes, I was getting worried, Butch. Goodness, what a large box of candies! I can hardly wait to sink my teeth into them.'

'Well, just take it easy,' he chuckled, watching her pluck at the adhesive tape and remove the wrapping. 'You don't want to make yourself sick on them.'

Mona lifted the lid and told him to help himself. He did so obediently and popped one of the candies into his mouth. He chewed.

'Yeah, these are good, sweetie. Kind of reminds me of the days we were courting.'

Mona put a candy into her mouth and demolished it speedily, smiling wickedly all the while. She was reaching for another one when she stopped short and screwed her face up.

'Say, what's wrong? You're not in the mood for candy after all, baby?'

'Not these, Butch. I — I — Oh, it was just a false alarm, darling. I'm sorry. But they're not as I imagined they would be. You know, you anticipate something and then it turns out differently from what you thought.'

'Sure,' he said weakly. 'I bought the wrong brand, huh? But I bought this brand for you lots of times before.'

'Bought?' Mona echoed as she replaced the lid on the box slowly. Her brow puckered up. 'But I understood that Mr Jones sent them with you, darling?'

'Yes, he did sure. A slip of the tongue.' Butch felt himself reddening. 'Just like me to want to steal somebody's thunder, honey.'

He took the box of candies from her and wrapped them roughly in the pink paper. No matter how he tried he could not rid himself of a feeling of dread. The sword was coming closer.

9

Frank Hartman's grey Volkswagen was parked close to the front entrance of Butch's bungalow when he arrived home from the hospital eventually. He had stayed for much longer than he had intended staying with Mona tonight, and he glanced at his wristwatch before switching off the headlamps. The time was nearing ten-fifteen and he was late for his appointment with the F.B.I. man.

But the way Hartman grinned and greeted him he was in no wise put about at the discrepancy.

'Hello, again, Butch,' he said in his cool, unruffled voice. 'How's the little woman making out tonight?'

'Pretty good,' Butch grunted. He had so much to think about now, and the sum total of the whole business seemed so utterly fantastic, that it appeared useless to hope that anyone could provide even a modicum of assistance. And what could an F.B.I. man do to help him, he wondered dismally. At best, cops were heavy-handed, and depended on the laws of reason and logic to solve problems rather on the incisive second-sight that was needed for this affair. He might be better off going straight to bed and getting some sleep than inviting Frank Hartman into his house to talk.

Hartman watched him remove the two small parcels from the driving seat of the Olds. He offered to hold them while Butch searched in his pockets for his doorkey.

'It's okay,' Butch said. 'I can manage. They're nothing but two boxes of candy,' he added to take the edge off the detective's curiosity.

'Imagine that now. You brought them to your wife, but she wasn't in the mood for candies?'

'Something of the sort.'

Butch let himself in and Hartman quickly shut the door on them. 'This guy Jones,' he said in a different tone of voice. 'He medium-built, with glasses, and wears a hat and rain-coat?'

'Yeah, that's him,' Butch answered, staring at the other in the hall lighting. 'What about him?'

'He came to visit. With you, that is. He seemed anxious to know who I was. I called myself a close friend of the family. He took the trouble to inform me that you'd gone to County Hospital to see your wife.'

'I see.' They were in the living-room now and Hartman fancied that the trucker had paled considerably. His eyes darted restlessly and he gave a hard bite to his underlip. 'What else did he say? How did he strike you?'

'He didn't say much else. He struck me as the meek, inoffensive individual you can find in any block, in any street, in town. But that doesn't fool me, Butch. I've known meek, inoffensive little men who sat crying their eyes out after slitting the throat of a wife or mistress who was two-timing or got boring.'

Butch's weak grin was meagre and whimsical.

'You know how it is, pal. Never judge the contents by the cover.' He had dropped the candy boxes on the table, and he proceeded to strip the coloured paper from the box given him by Alfred Jones.

'Something like that.' Hartman jiggled a little on his tiptoes, then rocked back on his heels. He cleared his throat. 'I'd rather have a drink than a candy if it's all the same to you.'

'I'm not offering you a candy, Frank. I'm right out of beer and I forget to get a carton. But you'll find a couple of bottles in the cupboard over there. One of whisky and one of gin. There'll be more whisky than gin, because that's Mona's tipple.'

'Your wife doesn't drink a lot, huh? Everything in moderation?' He was on his hunkers in front of the cupboard as he spoke. He brought out the bottle of whisky and held it up. 'Not bad. Enough to give each of us a cure.'

At this juncture Butch wasn't paying much attention to him. He was interested in the box of candies that had come from Jones. Once the wrapping was removed he whistled softly.

'What is it?' Hartman said, looking up.

'It's exactly the same. Can you beat it?'

'Uh-huh!' The detective wandered over with the bottle in his hand. He laid the bottle on the table and went off to the kitchen to fetch glasses. He was reciting a line from a poem when he came back with the glasses. ''Up the street came the rebel tread. Stonewall Jackson riding ahead . . . ' You know, they mightn't rank that as very slick verse, Butch. But it does have its points, don't you think? 'Halt! The dust-brown ranks stood fast. Fire! Out blazed — ''

'What the hell are you going on about?' Butch rasped at him. 'I thought you were supposed to be a detective. You sure you're not just another nut dreamed up by Jones?'

'Oh, Jones . . . ' Hartman chuckled and poured a measure into each of the glasses. He compared the measures and added a little extra to his own. He moved across and gave Butch his drink. 'Here, knock it back and slow down.'

Another outburst formed on Butch's lips but he choked it off. Hartman was grinning steadily at him and probing him with his bright, alert eyes.

'No, you're not nuts, Butch. But neither am I. Just because a guy behaves a little unconventionally at times you can't label him as a nut. Get me?'

Butch swallowed the whisky in two gulps and regarded him sceptically.

'What's that supposed to mean, Mr Hartman?'

'Call me Frank. It's supposed to mean this. I go around all day quoting bad poetry to myself. Another guy goes around magicing up busty dames out of thin air. You see what I'm driving at? We've all got our cudos and thingimyjigs. But it doesn't necessarily follow that we're nuts.'

'So I keep seeing things that aren't really there,' Butch retorted in a charged voice. 'Those cops told you everything and added a few frills of original invention. But still I'm not nuts? You followed me around in my truck today. What did you expect to see? I'd get out of the cab every mile or so and do handstands in the centre of the highway? But I wouldn't be nuts?'

'You're not reading me properly, Butch. I've got a job to do. I start at the beginning and take it from there. I want to see you in action, you understand. So I watch you in action. So I've seen you in action. But better still, I've talked with you, and I'm ready to get on to the next stage. What's up with the candies?'

Butch reached for the bottle that Hartman had laid aside, but he collected himself and brought a cigarette from his pocket instead. He flicked his lighter for the cigarette and rubbed the angle of his jaw while he puffed.

A cop, he thought. He talked like a cop and he behaved like a cop. The trouble was, he thought he was much smarter than the average cop. It really was a laugh.

'What's up with the candies? You didn't know what the parcel contained till you opened it?'

'I knew it contained candies.'

'You bought two of a kind?' Hartman frowned. He looked at the boxes and opened the one bought by Butch at the store up beyond the hospital. He saw where a couple of the candies had been extracted. 'Who ate these?'

'My wife had one and I had one.' Butch slumped down on to a chair and went on puffing at his cigarette. He expected Hartman to give him another verse of the poem. Instead, the detective sat down opposite him. He made a gesture with lean, delicate fingers which could quite easily have suggested that Hartman was a poet himself.

'Start right at the beginning. But before you do, Butch, where did you come by the candies? You took them to your wife, but she didn't like them?'

'That's right,' Butch said. 'This box here was given to me by Alfred Jones as a present for my wife. I took them to the hospital with me, but I remembered what happened when I brought Jones' roses to my wife last night, so I decided that she shouldn't have the candies.'

'Yet you bought another box,' Hartman nudged. 'Why was that?'

'I'll explain. But I'm doubtful that it'll do any good explaining. When I saw Mona tonight she told me she had a yen for candies. It — it was as though, by some means or other, Jones had instilled this longing for candies in my wife. I couldn't believe it. So I admitted that Jones had made a present of some candies and they were in the car. She asked me to go right down and fetch them. I went down to my car but I didn't bring up the candies. I couldn't risk Mona being ill again. You see, it happened with the roses . . . '

'Forgive me, Butch. I dropped you in the middle of the story. I should have let you start at the beginning. But you did bring roses last night from Jones, and as a result — At least, you imagine it was as a result of this that your wife became ill. Right so far?'

'Right,' Butch agreed thinly. 'But it wasn't a case of imagining anything. This actually happened. The roses got Mona hooked on the fragrance. Once she started smelling them she couldn't stop it. She became ill and they put a call through to me. But when I reached the hospital she was okay again. I met the nurse on the way in and she said it must have been the roses that upset my wife. Mona admitted how they had affected her, and when I left I spoke to the nurse again. She hinted that whoever had sold the roses had gypped me. She let me see them, and you know what? They had faded into nothing, almost. Just one look at them and I felt ill . . . '

His cigarette had gone out and Butch re-lit it. He did so with fingers that were none too steady. Hartman inserted a question.

'Why would Jones want to get at your wife? Granting that he really did want to get at her, of course.'

'There's no doubt in my mind what his game is. He doesn't want Mona to have our kid.'

For several moments after Butch said this Frank Hartman was silent. His gaunt features betrayed nothing of what was passing in his mind. But Butch knew what the detective was thinking, and on brief reflection he couldn't blame Hartman for labelling him as someone who had slipped his gears.

The silence ran on until Butch could

bear it no longer. He made a reckless motion with his hand.

'Go on and say it,' he urged with a trace of desperation in his tone. 'I ought to be locked up for my own good. For the good of the community. One of these days I might become violent, huh?'

The thin man brought a slow breath to his lungs and seemed to drag his concentration back from a great distance.

'Don't tell me what to say and what not to say,' he jolted Butch by stating. 'It's common for a guy to tell himself he's crazy once the going gets too tough for him. Going crazy is a nice handy way out of the mess. You've only got to make some nasty noises on a crowded street. Lie down and begin frothing at the mouth. After that the rest becomes easy. You — '

'Look,' Butch grated at him. 'I'm not frothing at the mouth. I'm not going anywhere to make nasty noises. But how the hell can I expect you to believe what those cops wouldn't believe? What no one in his right mind would believe.'

'There you go again,' Hartman reproved in his mild voice. 'You really have this thing about flipping. Just take it easy, Butch. Just get this into your skull for a start. 'There are more things in heaven and earth than are dreamt of . . . ' There really are, buddy, I'm telling you. Now, try to figure it from this angle. I'm here to talk to you, right? Help you if I can. It might extend further than that. I don't know if it could. But I want to find out. I'm keen to find out. I'm being paid to do a job. I don't hate my job. I don't hang around waiting for the hooter to go at the end of the day. Is that clear to you? If a case is unusual I'm interested. There's nothing I like better than the unusual. Not to say I'm some other brand of weirdo indulging his whim. The people who employ me wouldn't hire a weirdo. Do you understand all that, Butch?'

'Yeah, I do.' Butch sighed his gratitude. He was convinced that Hartman was genuine and sincere. He meant everything he said. An extremely agile brain was operating at the back of the easy-going façade he presented to the world.

'Now, you say that Jones doesn't want

Mona — your wife — to have a kid. Does what you think have any connection with a report in the day's issue of the Courier?'

'Then you read it?' Butch said eagerly. 'Yeah, I did see that report. My helper — Pete Rawlins — had a newspaper with him in Ferndale. I just happened to look at a page and there it was. The birth-rate in Caldwell has been falling during the past couple of years or so. Did it strike you as strange?'

'Somewhat extraordinary,' Hartman said in a non-committal manner. 'Extraordinary in that the pattern is not duplicated throughout the rest of the country.'

'And that could be bad?'

'Hold it right there,' Hartman said with a faint chuckle. 'I'm not an authority on birth statistics. I'm not an authority on any kind of statistics. A lot of people would say no, it's not bad: it's good. The world is gradually becoming over-populated. In a hundred years from now there'll be no room left for the people who are alive to move in. There won't be enough air to breath, enough food to eat. Well, in that event the problem might solve itself. But let's get back on to the rails, Butch. I'm putting it to you: why do you claim that this Jones guy doesn't want your wife to have her baby?'

Butch put another cigarette between his lips and lighted it. He puffed for a moment and marshalled his thoughts. In the present context, everything that had occurred seemed less fantastic. Having a sympathetic ear bent towards you made all the difference.

'Well, it all began this way . . . '

He told the detective of his first encounter with the stranger calling himself Alfred Jones at the hospital parking area.

'He had left his car in front of mine, and I was thinking what a thoughtless so-and-so he was when he came out of the hospital himself. Right off he greeted me by my first name. He led me to believe he had known me for quite a while. But I just let it ride and went about my business . . . '

He described how Jones had come into Wetzer's tavern on his heels, although he was certain that Jones drove off from the hospital in front of him.

'He left in front of you, but he arrived at the tavern behind you? It isn't possible Jones knew you would stop at the tavern and pulled up there to wait for you?'

Butch shook his head.

'There was a stream of traffic. By rights Jones should have been well in front of me on the road. When I stopped at the tavern I heard this other car drawing up. I know now it was his car. Even though he left in front of me he arrived behind me.'

'I see.' There was no trace of amusement or scepticism apparent in the sharp eyes that drilled into him. 'The guy was a total stranger to you until the minute he approached you at the hospital? He wanted you to believe he was an old acquaintance? He struck up a conversation in the bar?'

'That's what he did.'

Butch described how Jones appeared to know all about him and his wife. He could tell him the length of time he had been working for the State-Wide trucking company. He knew that Mona was expecting a baby, and knew, also, that the baby was overdue.

'Then he went into a spiel about the sorry state of the world and the tragedy of bringing babies into such a world. The guy figured it was a wrong thing to do. The adults in the world should be concentrating on making it a better place to live in before they ever thought of having babies.

'I admit he rattled me a little. Well, my wife was expecting our kid, and we'd always wanted a kid. You know how it is, Frank?'

'I guess I do.' Hartman shrugged and smiled faintly. 'I'm not a family man myself. I'm not even married. But I do have a measure of imagination. What then? You didn't know Jones was living on your street. Did he tell you that he was?'

'Yeah, he did. He said he was living in number twenty. I let it ride at the time. Like I say, according to Jones, he knew me well. I asked him what he was doing to make the world a better place to live in. And you know what he said?'

'What could he say to a question like

that?' Hartman countered with his brow puckering.

'He said he was doing his best. He put it to me that I might be in favour of leaning my shoulder to the wheel. I said why not, but my hands were pretty full as it was. He left the tavern shortly afterwards, saying he would see me around.'

'This stuff about the roses?' Hartman nudged. 'And at that stage it didn't occur to you to query that the guy was living on your street?'

'No, it didn't. That came the next night. I was leaving to drive to the hospital when Jones came along with the bouquet of roses. He asked me to give them to Mona with his compliments. I kind of softened to him then, naturally. The roses were beautiful. Mona thought they were beautiful. We got to talking about Jones, and the upshot was my wife had never heard of Alfred Jones either. She said number twenty was empty since Mrs Consby left. We both got a little worried, I suppose.'

'You suspected his motives on realizing

that he must be a stranger?' Hartman surmised.

'Wouldn't you have done the same? We tried to work out who he was. He might be a snoop from the trucking company. It seemed possible but highly unlikely. But if he wasn't after me for debt or after me to analyse my character, what the hell did he want with me? How come he'd gone to the trouble of finding out so much about me?'

'So you came home that night and drifted down the road to look at number twenty?' the detective hazarded.

'You're going too fast, Frank. I stopped off at the tavern when I left the hospital. Did you ever get a yen to taunt fate to do its worst on you?'

'But you didn't see him at the hospital when you visited.' Hartman frowned and got a cigarette going. 'He followed you into the bar, nevertheless?'

'He didn't have to follow me in,' Butch explained. 'He was right there when I arrived. He was sitting at the counter as if he knew I'd be along shortly.'

Hartman emitted a soft whistle. It was

plain he had never heard a story on a parallel with this one in his life before. He puffed a smoke ring ceilingwards.

'What did you talk about?'

'Jones was as smooth as syrup. He asked me how Mona was keeping. I put it to him that, as far as my wife was concerned, he was a complete stranger to her.'

'That hit him below the belt, I bet?'

'Not so you'd notice. He took it in his stride. He said he was sure he'd passed Mona on the street a hundred times without her giving him a glance. Then he said something that set me thinking plenty afterwards . . . '

'What was that?' Hartman asked tensely.

'He remarked that he might not be living on the street at all for the amount of attention he got from the people in the neighbourhood.'

10

Again Hartman emitted that soft whistle. He went over to the cabinet and poured two more drinks. He sipped carefully at his own drink while Butch swallowed the whisky in a single thirsty gulp. Butch wiped his lips, leaning forward slightly towards the other.

'Not only that,' he said. 'The guy had the nerve to tell me I'd be seeing plenty of him in the future.'

The detective's cigarette had gone out and he stretched across to drop it into the tray. He immediately brought a pack from his pocket and offered one to Butch.

'When you got home you went to see the house for yourself?'

'Not directly. I — ' Butch shuddered at the memory of the next link in the chain of events. But talking in this fashion to Frank Hartman was helping to bring the queer happenings into some form of perspective. 'You see the tree at the end of the driveway? Well, the first thing I noticed on getting home from the hospital was the way the tree seemed to be hanging ... Anyhow, there was a branch broken off my tree. I just couldn't figure it out. I was mad at the idea of someone harming my tree without any justification.'

'But kids could have done it, Butch. You know the way they get a kick out of fouling up things. They swing from ropes. They swing from tree limbs.'

'Not the kids on this street, Frank. There's another thing as odd as a guy with two left feet. A neighbour brought it to my notice. There are no kids as such on this street. Oh, kids right enough, but they've all grown up. What I'm trying to say is, there are no babies. As the neighbour said, having a baby would put Mona in a class of her own. But back to the tree. I got my flashlight and a ladder to have a look. The limb hadn't been broken the way it would be if somebody swung on it and cracked it off. It was a clean break, as — as if it had been sawed. But there were no saw marks in the wood.

I sawed through the smaller branches to release it. While I was up the ladder, friend Jones bobbed out of nowhere to see what I was doing. I damned near fell off the ladder when I saw the joker. This happened before I got the saw, you know. Hell, I'm getting mixed up, Frank. But it happened the way I'm telling you. Jones held the ladder till I came down. Then he said he'd better be going. He said it was time he was making out his re — '

'Come again,' Hartman said tautly. 'His what?'

'He didn't finish the sentence, you understand. It sounded like re — I got the notion he meant a report.'

'So now you got more curious about Jones?'

'You can say I did. I got to adding things up. Mona had claimed that number twenty Willow Road was an empty house. She said there was a 'For Sale' notice in the yard. I tried to forget it. But I couldn't forget it. Anyhow, I left our house and walked along to number twenty. I just had to get to the bottom of the mystery. If I didn't do something about it I might go crazy. I told myself I was probably going crazy anyway. Well, the sign was in the front yard. It said 'For Sale' and nothing else. The house looked empty and I went over to make sure. I went round the back and saw nothing there to alter my opinion. I headed for the front door and rang the bell. No answer. But I'd better tell you first that I looked in the garage and there was no car there either. But I shone my flash on the floor and there were oil drippings like you get from a sump or a faulty seal.'

'So you worked it out that somebody had been garaging a car, at any rate. The former resident didn't own a car?'

Butch shook his head.

He told Hartman about deciding to try his key in the lock of the front door. But the door had opened under a slight push. The house was empty. He knew it was, because he examined all the rooms. In the kitchen he heard mysterious noises. He had told the police officers of the noises and of the secret room that led off the kitchen.

'Yeah,' Hartman nodded. 'It was this

story about the room off the kitchen that really got me going, Butch. I've heard some screwball tales in my time, but this one took the cake. It's what prompted me to hunt you up. It was altogether too screwball to be an ordinary figment of the imagination. You saw a lot of instrument panels, and it was these which were giving off the noises?'

'I heard the noises,' Butch told him in a voice that had gone hoarse. 'I saw this instrument panel. There's not a single doubt in my mind that it was all there.'

'What did you do then?' the detective queried. 'Did you go into the room? Did you touch anything?'

'No, I didn't.' Butch rubbed his hands along his thick thighs. His eyes glistened, and a film of cold sweat was layered on his forehead. Hartman regarded him steadily, his own expression giving no inkling to his thoughts.

'What did you do, Butch? You raised the police department, I know. But before that?'

'Before that, nothing. I just turned tail and ran. Yeah, I did run, mister, and I'm not afraid to admit it. I never quit running till I reached this house.'

'Then you called the police department. Kinney and Jansen arrived. You told them everything and they took you down the street to Jones' house. But Jones was there by this time. Oh, yes, the notice telling folks that the house was for sale was in the yard. But there was a cancellation notice superimposed. That's so?'

Butch nodded. At this juncture his brain wanted to give up operating. He was aware of an onslaught of confusion. It seemed as though something deep down inside him was nagging at him, trying to warn him, urge him to be careful.

'And friend Jones answered the door to the cops? Jones brought you in and tried to make everybody feel at home. I asked Kinney if he made any explanation for the visit to Jones. He didn't, though. He decided to clam up until he'd heard your reactions. Do you know how Jones took the visit? He didn't ask you why you arrived there with two police officers?'

'He phoned me. But not right then.

When the cops left I had a call from the hospital. Mona was upset about something, it appeared, and could I drive out to see her? I drove out fast. When I got there she was okay. Sitting up in bed and apparently okay. But the nurse had mentioned the roses I'd brought her. She figured that the roses had caused Mona's upset.'

'How come?' Hartman asked in a tone that Butch scarcely heard. 'They weren't doctored?'

'How do I know?' Butch pulled his hands across his face. He thought the light in the room was growing too bright. A feeling inside him insisted that he bring the meeting with Frank Hartman to a speedy termination. Butch fought the feeling. 'Mona said that as soon as she started smelling the flowers she couldn't stop. Then she began to be ill and they brought the medico. The medico could make no definite diagnosis. He suggested that my wife might have developed an allergy on account of her condition. They removed the flowers from the ward and — and — '

His voice tailed off and Hartman sprang to his feet.

'What is it, Butch?' he cried concernedly. 'Are you all right? You aren't feeling sick or anything?'

'No,' Butch protested, loosening his shirt collar and glancing at the depleted whisky bottle. 'I'm not sure, Frank. I guess I'm getting mixed up.'

'Mixed up?' the detective echoed. 'But all this actually did happen? You didn't imagine it, did you?'

'No, no, I didn't. Give me another drink, will you?'

Hartman poured the remainder of the spirit into his glass. He stood over Butch as he gulped it down. Butch laid the glass aside and grinned wanly.

'I'm sorry.' He cuffed sweat from his forehead. 'It must be getting warm . . . Where were we?'

'The roses,' Hartman reminded him, lowering himself to the edge of his chair. 'Did you speak of your fears to the doctor?'

'I asked the nurse about the flowers. She showed them to me, and they had faded to nothing, like I said.'

'Fresh flowers fading in a matter of hours! I never heard anything to equal it. What did you do about it?'

'Nothing. But I see what you're driving at, Frank. I should have brought the flowers home. I should have offered them to the cops to have them analysed. But why should I, when the cops figured me for a nut?'

'Sure,' Hartman agreed drily. 'What happened when you got home? You say Jones rang you up?'

Butch nodded. He started to say something, but shook his head instead, his lips twisted ironically.

'What is it, Butch?'

'Nothing. Just a thought. Jones rang me and yet he doesn't have a phone — Hell, there's one way to check him out, Frank. If he doesn't have — '

'He isn't listed in the book,' the thin man informed him flatly.

'So you thought of checking for his number?'

'Yeah, I did. He isn't listed, like I said. I thought of something else as well, Butch.

I was in touch with the agent who had that house on his books. He sold the house right enough. He sold it to an Alfred Jones about two years back.'

'He did?' Butch groaned. 'Then that tears it, doesn't it?'

'Not necessarily. Oh, I know he could have rung you from a booth, and that would take care of the phone call. But there are plenty of loose ends that don't add up to keep me guessing. There's enough to keep me guessing for a year.'

'Then — then you actually do believe what I'm telling you? You've simply got to believe me,' Butch added passionately. 'Who else will listen to me, believe me? I couldn't tell Mona about the way I found the house empty, and about that room with the instrument panel. She's got enough to cope with, having the baby. She did want to hear more about Jones, though, but I brushed her off.'

Hartman nodded.

'You did the right thing in the circumstances,' he said. 'Where had we got to? You heard those noises in a room that seemed to have been built on to the kitchen. You really did see a room when you opened the door. Tell me this, Butch, did the sounds coming from the machines — or whatever they were — have any significance for you?'

'No, they hadn't. At the beginning I was too stunned to even think of trying to make out what was happening. There were just bleeps and clickings like the sort a computer would make. I simply got the wind up and ran. What would any average guy have done in the same position?'

'No doubt he would have run like blazes. Now we get to the point where Jones called you on the phone. This took place on your return from the hospital. What did Jones have to say to you?'

'He said he'd been trying to contact me earlier. I must have told him I'd been to the hospital. He asked how Mona was keeping, and it kind of slipped out about the roses and the way they had affected her.'

'You hadn't decided to take it up with him about the roses and the effect they appeared to have on your wife?'

'No, I hadn't. Not right then, anyhow. I

might have done it later, though. You see, I was confused. I couldn't understand how the flowers could have withered. Then . . . I didn't want to hurt Jones' feelings, you understand . . .'

Hartman's lips puckered. He had the impression that the trucker had taken just about as much as any man could take and still keep his reason intact. But he must continue to ask questions. The only way to get to the bottom of the mystery was to dig and keep on digging.

'How did he react to what you said about the roses?'

'He sounded horrified at the idea of the roses making Mona ill. I told him not to worry about it. It might have been something she had eaten that upset her.'

'Did you tell him how the flowers had withered when they were taken from the ward?'

'No, I didn't, Frank. Like I say, I didn't want to hurt his feelings unnecessarily.'

'Yes, I see what you mean, Butch. There was no proof that it was the roses. But he did seem anxious over what became of them ultimately?'

'I explained that they'd been removed from the ward and that Mona was all right afterwards. I didn't go into details. Then Jones switched the subject. The cops hadn't told him why they had visited at his house. He couldn't understand what I'd been doing accompanying them — '

'Did you tell him the truth?'

Butch smiled wryly, making a movement with his wide shoulders.

'You bet I didn't. I don't want to get poisoned in my sleep. Or maybe have my throat cut while I sleep.' He added seriously, 'I pretended to be as much in the dark as he was. I said they'd called here and searched around. Then they asked me to ride down the street to number twenty with them.'

'Did Jones swallow the guff, do you think? But if he's so smart it's hardly likely, eh?'

'I can't tell you, Frank. He figured the whole business was odd. He would see me around, or words to that effect.'

'Then? You tried to forget everything and went to bed?'

'I tried to. It was impossible. I kept seeing that empty house as I'd first seen it. Then I saw it the way it was when I entered it with the police officers. Would you have slept with that load weighing on your mind?'

'You didn't go back to the house?' Hartman asked tersely. 'But you did, by heaven! You've really got more nerve than I'd have credited you with, Butch.'

Butch's smile was mirthless.

'That's me all over. Nervy to the bitter end. Yes, I went back to number twenty, Frank. Do I have to tell you what I saw on that trip?'

'Hell, you're not saying the house was as you saw it the first time?'

'Just about, it was. But no, not quite. Anyhow, the notice was in the yard, but there was no cancellation sticker, like your pals, the cops, drew my attention to. Just the 'For Sale' notice. I went to the front window and looked in. Nothing. You know? All bare as Old Mother Hubbard's cupboard. I should have screamed blue murder and took off immediately. But I went to the door and pushed it and it opened like before. I called Jones' name to give him a chance to get his magic wand operating. No Jones. No magic wand being waved. I don't know how I did it, but I went on through to the kitchen. I didn't hear a sound coming through the door leading to the back yard. I opened the door. Nothing.'

'You — you didn't see this secret room?' Hartman queried in a voice that had a slight tremor threading it.

'No secret room. Just the back yard. As normal as it should have been.'

'You closed the door and went through the house to the front? You saw no sign of Jones on the way? The house was still empty?'

Butch explained that he had not gone through the house again. He would rather have done anything than gone back on his tracks. He broke off in mid-sentence and licked his dry lips. Hartman noticed the shadow that crossed his gaze now.

'That wasn't all, Butch?'

'No, Frank, it wasn't. I wished to hell it was. But of course this could have been a fluke. It might have been no more than a falling star, a shooting star . . . '

'A shooting star!' The detective's features were pale and tense. He leaned forward and made Butch look squarely at him. 'Go on and tell me about it.'

'What is there to tell?' Butch responded hoarsely. 'A star seemed to flash down at me. The light from it was blinding. I had to close my eyes when I tried to look at it. Then it faded and the sky was normal.' He saw the way Hartman was staring at him and gave a harsh laugh. 'That puts the tin hat on it, surely, Frank. I'm a screwball after all? The sooner they get me into a straitjacket and take me off to a padded cell the better for me, the better for Mona . . . and the kid. The better for everybody.'

'Take it easy,' the other urged soothingly. 'I didn't call you a screwball. But I do admit I've never heard the likes of it. I'll guarantee that nobody could match the story you've just told me. No, you're not crazy, chum. Far from it. Like I said, there are so many loose ends. More than I calculated there might be. Hasn't it occurred to you, Butch,' he went on vibrantly. 'This Jones character . . . He might not be human at all. He could be an alien from some planet out there in space. No, don't laugh, Butch. You should be the last person to scorn the idea. Just think of it. The way Jones can get around. The things he knows. The way the birth-rate has fallen during the past two years. And it's just happened in Caldwell, remember!'

'Holy smoke!' Butch breathed. The sweat oozed to his forehead and raced down his cheeks. 'So there was something queer about the roses after all. The candies . . . I figured he might have influenced Mona in some way. He's been going around, stopping babies being born. Now he's picked on us — me and Mona. Our kid. Our kid, Frank!'

'Easy,' Hartman repeated, gripping his arm. 'You've played it cool this far, Butch. You'll have to play it cool for a while longer. And listen, you keep everything that has happened to yourself. Don't tell your wife, even. Once it got to the newspapers there might be a panic. It could spread through the entire country.

A panic would suit Jones fine.'

'But what can you do about it, Frank? What can I do about it?'

'You string along with Jones as far as he takes you,' Hartman advised. 'Leave the rest to me. You've noticed that his house is occupied again? His car's there and the notice has been removed from the front yard. Whatever his game is, he intends to push his bluff to the limit. Well, let him, Butch. I'll get weaving immediately I get to the office. I'm going to take those candies with me for analysis, and I'll try to retrieve the roses you brought to the hospital.'

He rose, lifted the box of candies, and started for the door. He assured Butch that he would be in contact with him soon.

'Yes, all right, Frank. You've taken a big load from my mind.'

'Just keep calm,' were Hartman's parting words as he left the house.

Butch watched him go to his car and get behind the wheel. He waved and drove down Willow Road, heading for the south end of the street. He went from Butch's sight and he watched the rear lights of the Volkswagen. Then there was a mighty crash and the car seemed to somersault through the air.

11

For the space of ten seconds, perhaps, Butch stood where he was, petrified, staring through the gloom that shrouded the street and which was merely accentuated by the feeble glow of the lamps burning at each end.

A loud yell coming from somebody's throat thrust him into a spurt of movement. He began running down the road, hearing windows being thrown back, doors being opened. By the time he reached the scene of the crash there were half a dozen of his neighbours milling around, all wanting to do the right thing in the emergency, all rendered temporarily impotent by the nature of the accident.

Accident? Butch thought wildly as he gaped at the grey car turned upon its roof. The Volkswagen was in the centre of the road, and yet there was no other vehicle to be seen, no obstruction of any description whatever. So what had caused that almighty contact of steel jarring on steel?

Then he saw the figure of Alfred Jones bustling forward from the entrance to number twenty. The accident — or whatever you might call it — had occurred directly opposite the driveway leading to Jones' house.

Butch, with several other men — there were now at least a score of people at the scene, several women amongst them — hurried to the driving side door of the vehicle. Groans were issuing from the seat where Frank Hartman was trapped. Luckily for Hartman, he had automatically strapped himself in with his seat-belt; otherwise he would surely have been catapulted through the windshield and very possibly killed.

They clawed at the twisted door frame, smelling the growing stench of gasoline. At any instant the Volkswagen might erupt into a seething petrol bomb. Butch worked faster than the others, exerting all the energy he was capable of, clawing with a frenzy resulting in broken fingernails and torn flesh.

'Here's a crowbar,' Walt Burnheimer said, thrusting the implement into Butch's hands. 'Hey, some of you guys phone for an ambulance . . . '

'I've already done so,' elderly John Shearer said in a voice that quavered badly. 'Do you think he's alive?'

'Oh, he's alive all right. Who is he? What the hell did he hit? Tell me that.'

'I thought I saw another car on the road,' a new voice chipped in as Butch found a notch to insert the end of the crowbar. He recognized it as belonging to Alfred Jones.

'You did? Well, I didn't see a thing. I was just bringing my dog back from a walk. The car started from somewhere about your house, Butch . . . '

Butch vouchsafed no answer to this. Hank Stone was adding his weight to the leverage he had obtained. Jones continued talking, his tone gentle and regretful.

'There certainly was another car,' he declared. 'The way it looked, Mr — The gentleman here swerved to avoid hitting it. But he must have hit it.'

'Where did the guy take off to, huh? Nobody on this street would do a thing like that.'

'I didn't see a thing, I tell you. I was walking up my driveway with the dog. I'm not blind . . . '

'Can you make it, Butch? That gasoline sure stinks. She could go up in smoke any time.'

'Put your weight to this, damn you,' Butch hustled.

With the additional leverage the car door sprang open with a vicious snap. Butch was caught a numbing blow on the right elbow, but even this failed to deter him. He must get Hartman out of there fast. He must save Hartman. Part of himself was wrapped up in the detective, his hopes — the only hopes he had of fighting the sinister trap he was ensnared in.

He flung the crowbar aside and gained a grip on Frank Hartman's shoulder. He heaved and the detective's body began to appear.

'Are you okay, Frank? Can you hear me?'

A muffled croak was the only answer. With help he dragged the detective out clear from the car. They carried him over to the safety of the sidewalk and laid him down on his back. Two women were standing ready with blankets and they draped them on the inert figure.

Fingers touched Butch's arm and he turned.

'I'm so sorry about this, Butch. Truly I am. The gentleman was a friend of yours?'

The mild eyes glinted behind the spectacle lenses. By some trick of the poor lighting in the street, when Alfred Jones moved his head slightly the lenses became opaque. Just then Butch felt like gripping him by the throat and shaking him until he begged for mercy.

'What's the matter with you, Butch? You are shocked by the unfortunate accident? But of course you are. I am deeply shocked myself. Deeply grieved. I spoke to the gentleman earlier, you understand. I went along to your house and he was there. He appeared to be waiting for you to return from the hospital. How is your good wife this evening, Butch?'

'Mona was fine.'

'Good, good.' Jones sounded as if he meant it. He fingered his chin briefly and glanced down at the still form of Frank Hartman. 'He was a friend of the family, Butch?'

'Yes, he was.'

'How sad. But he may not be badly hurt. I trust he is not badly hurt. I believe he's attempting to say something, Butch . . . '

It was true. Frank Hartman had raised his head a little and was looking around. Butch dropped to his haunches beside him. Hank Stone was proffering a flask of brandy and Butch brushed the flask aside.

'You can't give him that, Hank. You can't give him anything till the doctors see him.'

'It's taking them a long time. But he's conscious at any rate, Butch. I guess he's going to live. Couple of bones broken, maybe, but what's a broken bone?'

Butch pushed him to the fringe of his

consciousness. He leaned over Hartman and saw that his eyes were open. The eyes were wide and glassy. They touched Butch without any trace of recognition.

'What — what happened?'

'It's okay, Frank. You had an accident in your car. You hit something. You must have hit something. You can't remember another car getting in your way?'

Hartman made a small negative gesture with his head.

'Where am I?'

'Quit worrying. You'll be all right. You don't recall seeing anything after you left me?'

'Who are you?'

When he said that Butch was aware of a lump of ice being laid against his spine. He glanced upwards sharply and saw Alfred Jones gazing sympathetically at them.

'Poor chap,' he murmured.

'You — you don't remember who I am, Frank? You don't remember what we said? What we talked about?'

Again that slight shake of the head. Hartman's eyelids fell. In the distance the wail of a siren lifted on the night air. It heralded the arrival of the ambulance in the locality, but it was several streets away yet, eating up the distance separating it from Willow Road rapidly.

Butch came slowly erect, his features grim. That haunted light was back in his eyes. If Hartman had lost his memory . . . If he should die . . .

'Amnesia,' Alfred Jones said in a low tone. 'But it might only be of a temporary nature. What did you say his name was, Butch?'

'Hartman. Frank Hartman.'

'A friend of the family?' The spectacle lenses reflected a smattering of light. The group of men in the roadway had succeeded in turning the Volkswagen upright. They pushed it away from the pool of gasoline that had formed. The atmosphere stank.

'I told you, didn't I?' Resentment roughened the words. Butch pulled a gulp of air to his lungs. The ambulance took the corner of the street on two wheels, siren crying like a demented soul, roof light flashing. 'You're sure you saw another car, Alfred?'

'Of course I'm sure. But it was too dark to determine what make of car it was. All I saw was its shape. I'm not too conversant with the various models there are, in any case.'

'The police will ask you,' Butch reminded him as the ambulance came to a halt at the kerb. Two police department automobiles slithered up in the wake of the ambulance. Officers began spilling out. A young intern leaped from the ambulance and came to make a cursory examination of the victim. He straightened after a moment and signalled for the white-coated attendants to get him on to the stretcher they carried.

'I can merely tell what I saw, Butch.'

An officer pressed forward and shot a glance at Butch and his companion before giving his attention to the detective.

'Why, it's Frank Hartman!' he cried. 'Get him to the hospital fast. Take him to Central, Doc.'

'Where else?' the intern said drily. 'I'll do what I can for him on the way.'

'You folks hang around, will you?' the officer said now. 'I'll want a statement from anyone who saw anything.'

'There wasn't much to see.' This from Alfred Jones who walked over to the policeman. He dropped his voice and Butch was unable to hear the rest of what he said.

The ambulance went off with the injured detective, siren baying once more, roof light flashing. Several of the police officers were now examining the Volkswagen in an effort to determine what, exactly, had caused the accident. A few of Butch's neighbours were talking to the officers, giving their versions of what had taken place.

Butch shivered slightly and looked towards the north end of the street. He could see no reason for holding on where he was. Something had taken place to put Frank Hartman out of circulation and that was that.

What? he asked himself as he trudged through the shadows to reach his own house. How could you crash your car into something that wasn't there?

It would have been different had Hartman swerved off the road altogether and struck a tree or one of the low, ornamental walls which a few of the residents of the street favoured. But to crash into absolutely nothing that had visible substance . . . How did nothing have visible substance? Could you have substance, or an object, that was not visible to the human eye?

'*Up the street came the rebel tread, Stonewall Jackson riding ahead . . .* '

The line of verse flitted through his brain from nowhere. He could almost hear Frank Hartman reciting it. Had he actually gone around quoting poetry to himself? Why not? Why should he not quote poetry to himself if it amused him? It might have been a method the detective used to relax or to help himself to think better when confronted with a problem.

'*Up the street came the rebel tread . . .* '

It was quite a while since the tread of rebel feet had been heard in this end of the world. Invaders, for that matter. Invaders! The word dug a groove in the layers of Butch's conscious thoughts and stayed there. Invaders from where? Invaders with what purpose in view? A drastic reduction of births all over the country? The eventual cessation of natural birth in the country? In the world as a whole?

The notion was too horrible to think about. It was the extreme of fantasy. It was utterly impossible.

Or was it?

Butch had left his front door open and he walked into the hallway and closed the door behind him. He made for the living-room and drank the last of the whisky in the bottle. Then he lighted a cigarette and threw himself into a lounging chair. There was nothing else to do but wait.

Sooner or later the police department would discover that Frank Hartman had been calling on him. They would want to hear everything that had transpired between them. Butch wondered if he ought to tell the police what he had told the detective. But no, it would be a mistake to tell the police what he had told

Hartman. The detective had advised against confiding in anyone — even his own wife. He didn't want the newspapers to get wind of it. And, naturally, if Alfred Jones was the sinister figure that events would have him be, then he must not learn anything that he could twist to his own advantage.

It was thirty minutes before the doorbell rang. Butch rose and went into the hall, thinking that the visitor might be the man from number twenty. But it was the police. Two officers stood looking in at Butch. The one nearest him inclined his head slightly and spoke.

'You're Butch — or Delmer — Deely, right?'

'That's me,' Butch agreed in a tired voice. 'What do you fellows want?'

'A word with you. Can we come in a minute, Deely? Your wife is in hospital, I believe?'

'Yeah, she is. Okay, come in.'

He shrugged and led them into the living-room. There was little resemblance between them and the officers he had entertained before. The one who did the talking was about fifty — a gnarled kind of a man who looked very tough and capable. His companion was a youngish coloured officer who just kept watching and making mental notes.

Butch made a gesture for them to be seated. They sat down and the older of the two crossed one lean leg over the other. He had no intention of beating around the bush.

'Frank Hartman was here at your house tonight, Deely?'

'That's so, he was.'

'You know Frank maybe?' This was accompanied with a probing stare that illustrated his puzzlement about such a connection.

'In a sort of way.'

'You're not very helpful, Deely, are you? You know, there's something about this that smells.'

'You're talking about the accident Frank had?'

'Frank, eh?'

'He told me to call him Frank. He was a nice guy. Don't get the idea he was checking me out on suspicion of maybe I planned to set a bomb under the White House.'

'So why was he checking you out? You had cops visiting not so long ago, Deely, right?'

'That's true. I thought I saw something unusual enough to be of interest to the police department.'

'That's right, you did. I didn't get the whole picture, but they'll have it at headquarters. What was the whole picture, Deely?'

'I just thought I saw something. I might have seen it or I might not. It's of no great consequence.'

'We'll find out if it is.'

'Yeah, you do that.' The coloured officer was smiling at him and he smiled back, thinly. 'What else do you want to know?'

'Why Frank was calling on you.'

'You'd better put that to Frank. I — '

'I'm putting it to you, buster,' the cop interrupted weightily. 'There's something funny about this. There's not a damn thing along the street that Frank could have crashed into. Do you know that, Deely?'

'I noticed,' Butch said, not looking at either of them. There was an air about him just then which impressed the officers. They exchanged glances.

The cop's tone softened. 'Have you got any idea what happened? Those chumps down the street only want to yak. They're yakking their heads off to a couple of press reporters at this minute . . . '

'Press reporters?'

'That's right. They might call with you. What will you tell them, Deely?'

'Nothing.'

'Nothing, because it's what you figure you know, or nothing on account of Frank Hartman. Frank was F.B.I.'

'So I believe. Nothing, I said. When Frank's well enough he can answer your questions. You guys have connections with the F.B.I.?'

'Of course.' There was a trace of sarcasm in the police officer's voice. He rose and his companion rose with him. 'You didn't see what Frank hit?'

'If I'd seen what he hit I'd tell you, wouldn't I?'

'A joker says he saw a car. What was his name, Bill?'

'Jones,' the other officer said from memory. 'Alfred Jones. He claims that Hartman swerved to avoid this auto. But he must have hit it, because there was a loud bang.'

'Did you hear a bang, Deely?'

Butch nodded. 'I heard it. I began running as soon as I heard it. But I didn't see a car. Neither did anybody else see a car.'

'Jones figures there was another auto involved. But never mind. The technicians can settle the matter. They'll take scrapings and samples, and the like. If another car was involved we'll have it tabbed this time tomorrow.' He paused and then said suddenly, 'You didn't go after Frank in your own car?'

'And deliberately crash into the Volkswagen?' Butch suggested angrily. 'Grow up, Officer. My car's at the front right now. Go over it with a fine comb if you care to.'

'Yeah, all right, Deely. I just figured I'd say it. There's no other information you wish to volunteer?'

'I'm sorry, no.'

Butch accompanied them to the door and let them out. He said so-long and watched them commence walking down the street. They talked to each other in low-pitched voices. He closed the door and went back to the living-room. He was there for five minutes when the doorbell rang once more.

He opened it on three men whom he took to be reporters.

'Hello, Mr Deely. We represent the Courier and the — '

'Sorry, fellows,' Butch broke in coldly. 'I've nothing to say to you. I can't tell you anything you don't already know.'

'But, Mr Deely, we thought — '

'I don't care a damn what you thought. I said what I said. Don't you understand the English language?'

'Sure, Deely, sure. Don't get sore. We merely thought . . . '

'Good-bye,' Butch snapped and closed the door in their faces.

Later, he could not remember when he had been so discourteous to anyone.

12

Butch sat waiting until well after midnight, smoking morosely and staring at the telephone. He expected the phone to ring and to hear Alfred Jones at the other side of the line. He expected a call from the County, asking him to hurry out there to his wife at once. He expected another visit from the police. Or the F.B.I. Or from Jones, thinking it would be much more convenient to talk to him face to face.

What would Alfred Jones want to talk about? About his entertaining Frank Hartman, no doubt. About the way the accident had occurred opposite the entrance to the driveway of number twenty.

How the hell had that accident occurred? How could he have heard the grinding collision of metal on metal when there was nothing on the road for Hartman's car to strike?

Had there really been another car involved and Alfred Jones was the only person who saw it? But why hadn't *he* seen it? Why hadn't the neighbour taking his dog home from a walk seen it?

'The police will soon get to the bottom of the mystery,' he mused. 'The police are no fools, despite what friend Jones might think of them. They'll be able to decide whether the Volkswagen was in contact with another car. But wait a minute . . . ' Butch wiped a layer of cold sweat from his brow. 'If Jones is able to furnish a house at will, and make it bare at will . . . If he's able to conjure up a secret room at the back of the house and make it disappear again, then what's to prevent him waving his magic wand — or whatever the devil he uses — and see to it that the Volkswagen is well smeared with paint splinters from another car?'

At around two o'clock Butch lay down on the couch and fell fast asleep. Sleeping, he was treated to a host of ghastly nightmares in which he and Alfred Jones figured. In one of these he saw Jones driving a car up and down the road.

He was laughing gleefully and shouting that he was on the lookout for F.B.I. men.

'You'd better leave the F.B.I. men alone,' Butch called frantically to him. 'What did they ever do to you?'

'They walked over my garden and trampled on my roses,' Jones appeared to retort with uncharacteristic venom. 'They trampled on the roses you took to your wife. You've as much right to make them crash as I have, Butch. Come along and join me.'

'No, no!' Butch cried. 'Frank says you're one of the rebels. You're the guy who fired that bullet at Barbara Fretchie. The rebels are coming down the street. They're invading us. They're going to grab all the kids from their beds . . . '

This merged into another fevered product of his subconscious.

He was standing at his front door, looking up at the sky where the stars twinkled and blazed in a rapture of coloured lights. In the dream Mona was standing beside him, with a bare arm round his neck.

'There is my star, darling,' Mona was

saying. 'Don't you see the big one that's smiling at us. It's coming here shortly and we're going to take a ride on it. It's taking us to see our son, Butch. Our son is up there, darling.'

'No, no, no!'

As he screeched savage denial a star blossomed into piercing bloom and raced from the heavens towards him. Butch squirmed and held on to Mona. Mona's arm about his neck tightened until he was unable to breathe. All the while she seemed to be laughing in a gay, abandoned fashion.

'Don't worry about the star, Butch. It's not a star at all, really. Don't you see, darling, it's Mr Jones with a bunch of beautiful roses for me . . . '

And so on and so on.

Daylight found Butch muttering in his sleep. He jerked awake and sat up, rubbing his eyes and whispering a fervent thanks for his deliverance.

Then the whole awful reality penetrated and caused him to groan in a spasm of fear and frustration.

'It all actually happened last night.

Frank Hartman was here. We did talk and I told him my story. Hartman believed me . . . Yes, he did. He believed everything I told him. And the car crash really did take place. Hartman was knocked unconscious. At least, he was knocked stupid. He failed to recognize me. He seemed to have forgotten what we talked about . . . Amnesia. Yeah, that's what it is. But he'll snap out of it and remember. He's simply got to snap out of it. Mona . . . '

He stumbled to his feet and went over to the telephone. He had to take a moment to arrange his thoughts in order to get the number of the hospital right. He dialled, wanting a drink. But not liquor this morning. He had never been a toper by any stretch of the imagination. Coffee. Yes, he needed some coffee. Lots of coffee, and it would have to be strong.

'County Hospital here. Can I help you?'

A wave of relief surged through Butch at the mere sound of those words. They were spoken calmly, from a sane and contained mind. So there really was reality and sanity in the world. It was simply a matter of finding the correct standpoint, of gaining the essential healthy perspective. Why, away from this house and this street they had never heard of a man called Alfred Jones. They knew nothing of the mysterious car crash down the road last night. For all the ordinary, unmolested people, knew, Alfred Jones might not exist.

The thought was wonderful and Butch Deely savoured it to the full.

'County Hospital here! Were you ringing?'

'Yes, yes, I was. I'm sorry. I'm Butch Deely. Delmer Deely. My wife's in maternity, and . . . '

'We know all that, Mr Deely,' the voice said with a slight tinge of amusement. 'If you'll hold on a moment, Mr Deely . . . '

'Yes, I'll hold on, certainly.' He laughed shortly. 'It's just that I'm kind of worried, you understand.'

'I understand perfectly. I'll inquire about Mrs Deely.'

'Thank you,' Butch said and waited. An age seemed to go past before the cool voice spoke to him again. But now it was not so cool. There was a quality of constraint in the timbre, Butch felt.

'Mr Deely . . . '

'Yes, I'm here. What is it? Don't tell me that the baby has been born! Is Mona — '

'If you could call again in ten minutes or so, Mr Deely . . . '

'But why?' Butch almost shouted into the mouthpiece. 'I mean, there's nothing the matter with Mona, is there? It's time I was getting ready for work, you see . . . ' He drew a quivering breath and willed himself to be calm. 'I'm sorry. All right, I'll hold on. You don't think I should drive to the hospital?'

'I can tell you nothing more at the minute, Mr Deely. If you'd just ring back in a little while.'

'Yes, I'll do that. Forgive me if I sound worked up. Yes, I'll call back again in ten minutes.'

There was a click and the line went dead.

Wait for ten minutes. Why the hell did he have to bear this suspense for ten minutes? Why couldn't they come right out and say if something was wrong?

What could be wrong? Were complications setting in that neither he nor Mona had envisaged or could have envisaged?

All right. He would give them ten minutes. But not a second longer than that. He glanced at his wrist-watch. It had gone eight-thirty. He should be at the truck depot by now. Being late for work two mornings on the trot would not please Cowan. But let Sam Cowan go climb a tree. It wasn't his wife who was in hospital. It wasn't he who was having to go through this misery of suspense.

Unless the message from the hospital was completely satisfactory and reassuring he would be out there in nothing flat.

Then he'd better shave and dress in something decent. His shirt was scruffy and his pants were rumpled. Mona would never forgive him if he didn't take the trouble to dress properly.

Butch was making for the bathroom when the telephone burred. He nearly fell in his haste to reach it and grab up the handpiece.

'Yeah . . . This is Deely. What — '

'Oh, hello, Butch,' the smooth voice of

Alfred Jones greeted him. 'I hope I'm not disturbing you too early in the morning. But I watched to see whether you were leaving for work. I — '

'What do you want, Alfred?' Butch broke in on him hoarsely. 'I'm kind of tied up at the minute. I overslept and I'm getting ready to go out.'

'I see. Forgive me, Butch. Very well, then. It's nothing of extreme importance, and we can easily talk about it this evening sometime. Good-bye for now, Butch.'

'No, wait,' Butch choked. 'If you make it snappy I'll listen to what you've got to say now. What is it, Alfred?'

'Nothing of great consequence, I'm sure, Butch. It's merely this . . . Remember that box of candies I offered you to take to your wife at the hospital?'

Holy smoke! He'd forgotten all about the box of candies. Frank Hartman had taken them with him last night in order to have an analysis run on them.

His voice throbbed when he spoke.

'I remember, of course. What about the candies?'

'Well, strangely enough, Butch, I happened to glance out to the street this morning — not long ago, in fact — and I saw an object in close to the kerb, just about opposite to where Mr Hartman had his unfortunate accident . . . '

'So what?' Butch urged hollowly when Jones appeared to make a pause for breath. He could feel his heart hammering painfully against his ribs. It was as though Jones could keep one move ahead of him, as if his view was much wider and his assessment could be made more rapidly. He saw the stranger as a man with a chart laid out in front of him. He was equipped with a red pencil and he was making lines all over the map: not lines which he, himself, intended following, but rather which he would dictate as routes for other people to follow.

'You can't guess what that object was, Butch?'

'No, I can't.' If he expected Butch to betray fear or apprehension he was due for a let-down. A man can be pushed just so far, made to take just so much. The moment comes when he bares his teeth and squares his shoulders and yells at the world to do its worst. Perhaps there would be a reaction later, but at least it would have been demonstrated how he was the keeper of his own soul.

'It was the candy box, Butch. The exact — or a startlingly similar — box that I gave to you to take to your wife.'

'Oh,' Butch said. 'So how did that come about, Alfred? You're saying that Mr Hartman had this box of candies in his car with him last night? If he did it was a box of his own that he had. It sure wasn't the one I handed to Mona.'

'Then you gave the candies to your wife, Butch?'

'Yes, I did. Look, I'll have to go, Alfred. Why make a fuss over such a simple thing?'

'Of course, of course! Why indeed? But not knowing who the real owner of the candies is, I'm undecided as to what to do with them. I never eat candies, Butch.'

'Me either.'

'I'll not detain you for any longer, Butch. I hope poor Mr Hartman was not seriously injured. The police officers questioned me concerning the car he struck opposite my driveway. They don't know what to think of the business . . . '

'One thing you can bet on, Alfred. They won't sit around making wild guesses. They'll give the Volkswagen to the fellows at the lab, and they'll take it apart, searching for clues. They'll be able to say what sort of car rammed Hartman or what sort of car he hit. If he really did hit a car, that is.'

'You doubt my word on the subject?' Jones asked in horror. 'It's the very last thing I expected of you, Butch.'

There he goes again, Butch reflected grimly. Pushing him into a corner. Wanting to make out that he's so timid and gentle he wouldn't hurt a fly.

'I didn't say that, Alfred. I'm merely saying how the cops will approach it. They deal in facts.'

'Naturally, they do.' He gave a short laugh. 'I find you so interesting, Butch. We must get together soon for a real chat. I find your company so stimulating. Good-bye for now, Butch.'

Butch grunted good-bye and hung up.

He knew that his forehead was gummy with sweat, and he knew without looking at his hands that they were shaking slightly.

Hartman, he thought now. If he rang the Central would they tell him what the detective's condition was this morning? Yes, they might, and it was worth a try. By now the F.B.I. man might have snapped out of the shock he had sustained last night. He might not be seriously injured.

But first he had to decide whether he was turning in for work today. At this minute Sam Cowan would be having a fit. He could visualize the manager striding up and down the yard, hands grasped behind his back. And if it developed that he must make the journey to the County Hospital, then he could not turn in for work today in any case.

Butch glanced at his wristwatch before dialling the truck depot number. Five minutes had slid by since he'd spoken to the person at the hospital switchboard. And he'd still got to clean himself up and change.

'State-Wide transport service!' Miss

Keith's voice spoke from the office in the depot.

'Hello, Miss Keith. This is Butch Deely speaking. Would you mind telling Mr Cowan that I won't be in today?'

'Yes, all right, Butch.' The girl's voice brightened. 'Don't tell me that the happy moment has arrived, Butch? Has the baby been born? Oh, I'm so — '

'No, there's no news yet,' he interrupted her. 'At least there's no definite news. I made a call to the hospital, you see, and they want me to ring back.'

'Then there must be something in the pipeline, Butch. You're worried about it, eh? Well, try not to worry. Everything will turn out fine in the end.'

'Sure,' he said with a forced chuckle. 'I sure hope so. Then you'll put Sam in the picture?'

Miss Keith said she would do so at once and Butch thanked her and broke the connection.

By now it was a toss-up between calling the County and getting in touch with Central regarding Frank Hartman. Butch hesitated only briefly. He pulled the phone book over and flipped the pages until he had the number he needed. He dialled and as he did so he muttered a fervent prayer for the condition of the detective.

'Central Hospital,' a youthful male voice said in his ear. 'Go ahead, please.'

'I'm — uh — inquiring about Mr Hartman who had an auto accident last night. Could you tell me how he's making out this morning?'

'That would be Mr Frank Hartman?'

'Yeah, that's right.'

'Hold the line, please.'

A few seconds passed and then a hard, business-like voice greeted Butch.

'Hello! You're asking how Frank Hartman is this morning. Would you give me your name, if you please?'

Immediately Butch realized what had happened. The operator at the hospital switchboard had given the nod to a nearby police officer. It showed that they thought there was some mystery attached to the incident on Willow Road.

Butch had an urge to lay the handpiece back on its rest and let the thing ride. But that would serve nothing useful. It would be a matter of minutes before the police ordered a check on the caller. They would trace the call to his address, when unwanted complications could ensue.

Butch touched his dry lips with the tip of his tongue.

'My name's Delmer Deely. I suppose you know that Hartman had visited with me last night, just before the accident happened?'

'Yes, that's right, Mr Deely. My name's Holbrook, and I'm a colleague of Hartman's. I intend to call on you some time today, when it's convenient for you.'

'Yeah . . . Well, that's okay by me. But what about Frank? Was he done up badly?'

'Not too badly, thank heaven. Bruised ribs and a busted collarbone. Then he did take a slight injury to the head. The X-rays show that his skull's okay, but he appears to be suffering from some degree of concussion.'

'I see. Yes, I thought he had hurt his head. Can — can he remember what happened to him last night?'

'Well, he just came round about an hour ago. The doc won't let anyone talk to him for more than a minute. But I got the impression that he's suffering from a loss of memory. Look, Mr Deely, when would it be convenient for me to call? There are one or two things I'd like to tie up.'

'You'd better wait until later in the day. Say the afternoon if it suits you.'

'You're not at work, Deely?'

Butch explained that he was waiting to hear news of his wife at the County. His wife was expecting a baby that was overdue, and he was going to take the day off and sit it out.

'Okay, Mr Deely. We'll let it go at that. I'll ring you some time in the afternoon and make a date. Hope you get good news of your wife.'

'Thanks.' Butch laid the receiver on its rest. He had another look at his wristwatch on his way to the bathroom. The ten minutes were up. It was more like fifteen minutes since he had spoken to the switchboard girl at the County.

The telephone rang.

Butch wheeled and grabbed the

receiver, announcing himself in a flat, constricted voice.

'Mr Deely, could you come to the hospital at once? The doctor would like to see you.'

'What! Something's wrong . . . Something's happened to Mona!'

'Don't alarm yourself, Mr Deely. Your wife is all right. But the doctor would like to talk to you.'

'I'm on my way,' Butch replied and hung up.

He raced from the house as he was and slammed into the Olds. He drove, flat-out, up the long hill winding to the County Hospital, ignoring the angry blares of auto horns, the fist-waving of the drivers he stormed past with nothing to spare.

On reaching the hospital, he parked opposite the entrance doors. As he hurried to the elevator it reached ground level and a doctor whom he recognized emerged. He smiled weakly at Butch.

'Your wife has pulled through, Mr Deely. But I'm sorry to tell you it was impossible for us to save the baby girl . . . '

13

Butch rose at dawn that morning. He flung the bedclothes aside and felt around on the rug for his slippers. His feet encased, he came to the floor, stretched and yawned. There was a slight chill in the air, he imagined. He had switched off the heating before going to bed and the house felt cold, desolate. Much like the way Butch felt himself.

Butch went into the bathroom, shaved, showered. Dressed, he regarded his reflection in the shaving mirror once more. What he saw there did nothing to reassure him. It was no use kidding himself. He had taken a bad beating during the past three days, and the ravages were there to be read — in his dark-circled eyes, in the host of fine lines that were finding depth in the weathered flesh beneath the eyes and at the corners of his mouth.

Seldom had Butch Deely indulged in

critical self-examination on a physical or psychological basis. Were someone to have asked him for an assessment of his own personality he might have said he considered himself to be an extrovert, outward looking and appreciative of the sights and sounds and the other sensations which stimulated consciousness and kept it alive. But gradually he could see himself turning inwards, asking questions that, a short time ago, would never have occurred to him.

'Why me? Why did this have to happen to me? What is so special about me? Why have I been picked out for this sort of worry and anxiety and fear? Why my kid? Why Mona . . . ?'

Well, she had borne up better than he had ever thought she would. But women always did manage to surprise you. Men were supposed to be tougher, to be equipped with a thicker hide and a greater degree of resilience of spirit. But that was not so. The men were the weak sisters when it came to the pinch. He had wanted a son. He had begun shaping his life from that viewpoint. A new, precious segment was being introduced to the context he operated in. A girl had been born to Mona. Stillborn. Three days ago. An eternity and yet a mere thought and breath away.

They said that Mona could come home at the end of the week.

At first he had seen this as the end of everything. Mona would sink deeper into the depression that assailed her, and he wouldn't be able to do anything to help her find her feet again. And yet, on the second day afterwards, she had sat up in bed and held his hand, gazing deeply into his eyes all the while.

'I'm sorry, Butch. Can you ever forgive me?'

'Forgive you? Honey, what sort of talk is that? Me forgive you! Just — just because our . . . ' He had been unable to finish and the pressure of her fingers intensified. He had felt like breaking down and crying, but those tensile fingers had lifted him out of his misery. The softness of her tear-damp eyes contrived a cushion which he allowed himself to sink into gratefully. Where could you ever find another woman like his Mona?

'It isn't the end of the world, darling. It isn't the end of anything. We'll just have to look at it so. There'll be another day, another time . . . Yes, darling, the doctors have assured me of this.'

'Thank heaven,' Butch murmured fervently.

Everyone had been the soul of sympathy and helpfulness.

On getting back from the hospital that afternoon, Andy Midgley and Mel Krantz had come to the front door. It was a moment when he didn't want to see anyone, and by some twist of his imagination he saw his neighbours as arriving to gloat over his misfortune. They might have said, in effect, if our wives can't have any more kids then your wife can't have one either.

He had been cold and hostile to the two men until Mel Krantz revealed that practically all his neighbours on the street had got together a month ago to arrange a mammoth birthday party for the new baby.

At this revelation Butch could have

cried on their shoulders.

'I'm sorry fellows,' he had gulped. 'You make me feel like the biggest heel in the world. That was real nice of you. It was real nice of you, fellows . . . '

'Forget it, Butch,' Mel Krantz said gruffly. Then he gave a short laugh. 'It wouldn't have been planned as a completely unselfish gesture, Butch. It would simply have given all the women-folk on the street a ball. Well, women love kids. They love having them and raising them. But what's gone wrong with everybody?' he asked in a pseudo humorous fashion. 'I can tell you that we're not against having babies. There's nothing we'd like better than to have another baby. Phyllis tells me that at least a dozen of her pals think the same way. But the kids don't happen any more. Did you see the piece they ran in the Courier the other day? Would it be the air in the town, do you think? Or the water we're getting? We've talked to the family doctor about it, but he can't offer any clue to the problem or any solution to it.'

'Yes, it's queer,' Butch had agreed in a

flat, lifeless tone. 'There might be some reason. But they say the authorities are working on it. They're qualified to do this sort of research. They might come up with the answer eventually.'

Afterwards, Butch had smoked cigarettes and thought of Alfred Jones.

That day, too, there had been another communication from the man called Holbrook. Would it be all right if he visited at his home around six in the evening?

Butch had explained about Mona and the baby, and advised Holbrook that he was not up to talking today.

'You'll have to give me a while to settle down, Mr Holbrook.'

'Of course, Mr Deely, of course. Look, I'm very sorry to hear the bad news, Butch. I'll tell you what. I'll give you a number to call when you pull yourself together.'

He had given him the number and Butch had made a note of it. He asked about Frank Hartman's condition and learned that the F.B.I. man remained poorly.

'You mean he can't remember things clearly yet? He can't remember how the accident happened?'

'I mean exactly that. Physically, he's not bad at all.'

Butch had waited for a phone call, or a visit, from Alfred Jones, but during these three days he had heard nothing from Jones, nor had he seen him abroad on the street.

* * *

In the kitchen, Butch made a pot of coffee and prepared some toast. He forced himself to eat the toast, as his intake of solid food recently had been practically nil. Sam Cowan had told him to take a week's leave of absence on full pay, but he fancied he might have been better off working. He would have had less time to think about himself and his appetite might have improved. On the other hand, he wanted to be free to visit Mona at the hospital at a moment's notice. Although his wife appeared to be bearing up well, the doctor had informed him of the possibility of a belated reaction.

It was another of those fine, clear mornings as Butch left the house eventually and drove the Olds to the street. He would drive to the County first of all and stay a while with Mona. Then he had the notion to visit at the Central in the hope of being permitted to see Frank Hartman.

Obeying a whim, he turned left to reach the south end of the street instead of leaving it by the more convenient north end. He wanted to have a look at number twenty and assure himself that Alfred Jones continued to occupy the house.

At this juncture he had the fear that Jones might have packed his things and moved out of the district. After all, if only a small measure of his theories were correct, Jones' work should be finished in this end of town.

Even if Jones had moved or intended moving, there was absolutely nothing he could do about it. Going to the police with a request that they restrain the bespectacled man somehow was out of the question. How could he expect anyone to believe the fantastic theories he harboured concerning Jones? It might all have been different had there been no accident involving the detective. Frank Hartman had believed everything he had said regarding his experiences with the stranger, but Hartman was one person in a thousand. Butch had considered summoning Holbrook and repeating the tale to him, hoping that he would be as intelligent and receptive as his comrade. But he could not bring himself to phone and set the ball rolling. He wanted to forget the episode with Alfred Jones, pretend, if he could, that it had never taken place. And yet, if he did that, he would be shirking his responsibility to the rest of the people in Caldwell, and perhaps, indeed, to the entire population of the country.

There was the other side of the coin, also, to be considered. Frank Hartman had urged him to keep their conversation a secret. Whether this was supposed to take unforeseen circumstances into account he could not say, naturally, and had Hartman imagined he was scheduled to be put out of action it was possible if not probable that he would have wished to make suitable counteracting provision. In any case, Butch was reluctant to extend his confidence beyond Frank Hartman.

He drove slowly past the front of number twenty, aware of an increase in his pulse rate as he did so. Yes, the Ford was parked yonder opposite the garage. There were curtains on the windows. The door of the house stood open, although there was no sign of Alfred Jones anywhere.

Butch reached the end of the street and went into the wide detour he would have to make now in order to take up the road leading to the hospital. He was sweating slightly and a cold anger had begun churning in his veins. So Jones fancied he was sitting high and dry, removed from all suspicion and any form of retaliation.

Retaliation.

The word lodged in Butch's brain like a well-planted seed. There was something to consider without doubt! And why should he not plan some retaliatory action against the man who had robbed him and his wife of their baby?

'But it all sounds so crazy,' he muttered. 'How can I be sure that it actually did happen the way I figure it did? Maybe the whole business was nothing more than a series of hallucinations . . . '

It was possible, Butch decided from the depths of cold reason and logic. Alfred Jones might be nothing more than he had thought he was at the outset — a harmless crank with a bee in his hat concerning the state of the world and its unfitness for the introduction of innocent babies. He could have imagined he saw that stark 'For Sale' notice in the front yard of the house. But the cancellation sticker had been there all the time. He could have imagined that the house was bare and empty on the two occasions when he appeared to discover it so. The house hadn't been empty: it had been furnished as Jones ordered it furnished. The mysterious room at the rear was another hallucination; so was the brightly shining star whose flare had disturbed him to the point of panic.

Then he must admit that the trouble lay with him and not with Alfred Jones. He had sampled the initial encroachment of a mental break-up. The roses and the candies had been invested with sinister elements that had no substance outside the realms of his feverish imaginings. The tree branch had simply broken off.

'But the roses died,' he whispered in a savage outburst of rejection. 'They were not normal roses at all, not natural roses. They were something cooked up by Jones to further his purpose, his scheme. And the crash that Frank Hartman had . . . What did he crash into when there was no other vehicle in the road that night?'

Yet this was a question which Frank Hartman, only, could answer.

He must see the F.B.I. man. He must do all in his power to assist the detective in the recovery of his memory. Without the F.B.I. man at this crucial stage he was lost.

Mona was up and about when Butch reached the hospital. He found her in the TV room, and she came towards him with a welcoming smile on her face.

'I just knew you'd be here early, Butch,' she said, kissing him on the cheek. Then she stood off slightly to regard him critically. 'You've lost weight, you know. Too much weight, darling. What did you have for breakfast this morning?'

'Bacon and eggs.' He grinned and led her to a quieter part of the room. An old thriller film was being shown on the TV and the staccato exchange between the hero and the leading baddie struck an incongruous note.

They took chairs by the window overlooking the hospital driveway and parking area. Mona giggled and pointed out their car.

'It could do with a wash, Butch. But I suppose that'll have to wait, also, until I get home.'

'Why? What else has to wait?' He let her take his fingers and play with them.

He felt that he just wanted to relax here with his wife and think of nothing. Mona had an ability to soothe him and put his worries into their proper perspective. And what worries could he have so long as she was fit and healthy, and would soon be back home to look after him?

'Feeding you properly, that's what. You're getting as skinny as a rake. That paunch you were developing is practically non-existent.'

Butch made a face at her.

'Leave my paunch out of it. I never had a paunch, anyhow. So I might not be stuffing myself the way I used to. So what? I'm going to be much cuter to handle.'

They looked into each other's eyes and Mona's features sobered. She had a grip on his index finger and she was stabbing it slightly with her nails.

'I'd like to get home right now, Butch. You know that, darling. All I want to do now is get home as quickly as possible.'

'You don't have to rush it. You went through a rough time, you know.'

'Yes, I do know.' Her full lips

compressed for a moment. Her eyes fell, displaying those long, silken lashes. Then she looked directly at him again. 'But it's over, darling, and I'm going to tell myself that I've no regrets.'

'That's the best attitude to adopt, sweetie.'

'You've had it rough, too, Butch. Oh, you don't have to take the trouble to deny it . . . Tell me this,' she said, suddenly going off at a tangent, 'have you seen anything of that queer gentleman lately?'

A shudder took Butch which he tried to conceal. A faint smile warped the mobile thrust of his lips.

'No, I haven't seen him lately. Not since — Not since he gave me the box of candies for you.' He had told her nothing of the visit of the police or Frank Hartman. She was in the dark regarding the accident suffered by the detective. It was possible that one of their neighbours would bring her up to date, of course. But until that time came he was going to keep quiet.

'What a shame it was, darling. Not being able to eat the poor man's candies.

And those beautiful roses . . . They just overpowered me in some way.'

'Did — did the nurse tell you what became of the roses?' he asked her hoarsely.

'What became of them?' Mona echoed, illustrating her ignorance and causing Butch to regret the query. Her eyes narrowed. 'What do you really mean, darling?'

'Nothing.' He shrugged carelessly. 'They took them to another ward, didn't they? You didn't hear of them overpowering anyone else?'

'Well, I should hope that they didn't. Butch, I — ' She broke off and lowered her eyes again fractionally. She seemed to be fumbling for the right words to say.

'Go on,' he nudged. 'You were going to tell me something. Not about the roses?'

'No,' Mona said and bit her underlip briefly. She released his fingers and clasped her hands together on her lap. 'It's to do with me, Butch. The baby — '

'I told you to forget the baby,' he chided in a passionate whisper. 'It's over and done with. It happened like it did and we can't mend it. I thought you'd got over the shock and the disappointment.'

'Yes, I believe that I have. You imagine you're a realist, darling, but I'm every bit as much of a realist as you are. I'm not talking about myself now, but about three other women who were in maternity with me . . .'

'What happened?' Butch queried in a voice that shook a little. 'Their husbands didn't present them with flowers that — '

'Of course not. At least, I've no way of knowing whether they did. I'm sure they did. But that has no bearing on it. The plain truth is, Butch, that they lost their babies in the same manner.'

Had she struck Butch in the face the effect on him could not have been greater. For several seconds he merely sat, gaping at Mona and wondering if he was hearing her aright. A sensation of icy chill touched the region of his spine.

'Are you sure of that?' he blurted out at length. 'I mean, somebody didn't just tell you that to make your own disappointment less keen?'

'No, it's true enough, Butch. We aren't

the only couple who have had the bottom torn out of their lives. There are rumours circulating through the hospital, it seems. According to one report I heard, they've emanated from the doctors themselves.'

'What sort of rumours?' Butch croaked. 'Concerning the stillborn babies?'

'Yes. It appears that the local paper featured an article on the drop in the town birth-rate. I tried to get a copy, but no one seemed to have one. Did you happen to see the feature? It was in the Courier several days ago.'

Butch said that he had not seen the article in question. He had not heard it being discussed anywhere.

'No, I dare say you wouldn't hear men discussing anything so important to women,' Mona retorted with a faint smile. 'But it could be important, and I'll keep my ears cocked for further instalments.'

'Yes, you do that, sweetie.'

For once he was glad to take his leave of Mona and ride down in the elevator to the foyer. On his way to the Olds he heard a window being rapped and looked up to see Mona waving at him. He waved and strode on to the car. He kept waving at his wife until he could no longer see her framed in the window.

* * *

At Central they permitted him to pay a short visit to Frank Hartman, and after being directed to the ward where the detective was located he set off to find it. He was surprised to see a tall, huskily built man seated on a chair outside the ward door. He rose and introduced himself, assessing Butch shrewdly.

'Jud Holbrook . . . Yeah, I thought you were Deely. I'm pleased to see you, Deely. You might do something to jar Frank's memory. Oh, yes, he's able to have visitors. But wait a moment, Butch,' Holbrook added as a thought occurred to him. 'I guess it'll do no harm to tell you of the tests we ran on the Volkswagen. There was no trace of anything apparent to suggest that Frank crashed into another auto.'

14

Frank Hartman was propped up in bed with the lower part of his chest bandaged and his left arm in a sling to make it easier for the broken collarbone to knit. He had paled somewhat under his naturally dark complexion, and his lean face seemed more gaunt than usual.

It was incongruous, Butch thought, that Holbrook had to introduce him.

'You remember this guy, Frank?'

'No, I don't know him.'

'Well, his name's Deely and he lives at Willow Road. You know? Where the crash happened.'

Hartman smiled faintly, his eyes level on Butch, running over him wonderingly.

'You know I can't remember any crash, Jud. Yes, they tell me I was involved in an accident. My car hit something and I took a beating round the skull. I must have been in an accident to get myself wrapped up the way I am. For the rest, no dice.'

'If you'd leave me alone with Frank for a while,' Butch suggested, taking the chair by the bedside indicated by Holbrook.

'It's what I'm doing. Is it okay with you, Frank? From what I've heard, you ought to know Deely better than I do.'

'Yeah, it's okay with me, Jud. Go on and leave us together.'

He sighed and grinned sheepishly as Holbrook quit the room. There was a hint of medicaments in the air. There was a distinctly clinical air about this place. Butch couldn't help thinking that it was quite different from the County. Only, Mona had been in the maternity wing there. Medical and surgical wards did have a distinctive aura.

Hartman said, 'Would you mind getting my cigarettes out of that locker drawer, Mr Deely? Thanks,' he added as Butch produced the cigarette pack and handed it over to him. 'They frown on smoking in this neck of the woods. Here, help yourself.'

'I'll not smoke now,' Butch told him. 'You really don't remember me, Frank? My name's Butch.'

'I'm sorry. Honestly.' Hartman flicked his lighter and puffed. He dragged tobacco to his lungs as though he had been deprived of the luxury for some little while. His dark eyes lingered on Butch, troubled at his inability to recall him. 'You come from Willow Road, Jud says. I'll be more than grateful if you can help me surmount this damned obstacle, Butch.'

Butch nodded, aware of a sinking sensation in the pit of his stomach. This visit to the F.B.I. man could prove completely abortive; it might amount to nothing better than a waste of time. And Butch was convinced that there was no time to spare. As he saw it, Jones had moved into the open to a large extent. He thought himself unassailable and invincible. He thought he could bluff his way to the limit, without harassment or even challenge.

Butch recalled what Hartman himself had suggested concerning Jones. He might be an alien from some other planet. And he could be exactly that, with his avowed aim the ultimate destruction of all mankind. It was enough to make anyone quake.

'I'll do what I can, Frank. You can't remember anything? How you came visiting at my house, how we talked . . . '

Hartman shook his head. He mustered a smile, but the expression on the truck driver's features made him sober.

'According to the way you look, Butch, getting my memory back is pretty important to you. Well, I've the feeling it's as equally important to me. You could quite easily take Jud into your confidence, you understand. This involved the sharing of confidences?'

'Of course it did,' Butch cried passionately. 'I had all my hopes pinned to you, Frank. I was sure you could help me out of the mess. I don't want to take Holbrook into my confidence. It might be a big mistake. He isn't like you. Anyhow, you made me promise to keep it to myself. You advised me not to tell my own wife.'

Something akin to pain was mirrored briefly in the detective's gaze. It was obvious to Butch that Hartman had been striving mightily to jolt his memory back to normal, without any success.

'I'll tell you what I know,' he said slowly from taut lips. 'I remember that I had an assignment to cope with. I remember driving into Willow Road, but after that, nothing.'

'You don't recall being at our house? I talked to you about my wife, Mona. She was in hospital expecting our baby. I talked to you about Alfred Jones . . . '

'Yes, they've told me about Jones. They've told me about you, Butch. You called the police to investigate this house that Jones lived in on Willow Road. You saw things that weren't there, and you didn't see things that should have been there. Right?'

'That's it,' Butch said. 'After we talked you got into your car and drove down the road. I heard a crash and figured you'd hit another auto. But there was no other car on the road. Did you see anything on the road ahead of you, Frank?'

'I don't remember,' Hartman said with an edge to his tone. 'My memory's okay up to the minute I drove into the street.

After that blank. I don't know why you wanted me. But you didn't send for me, did you? I heard the tale from the police and took it from there. I must have been curious.'

'But if you remember everything up to the time when you drove into the street, you must remember how you followed me around in my truck. You tailed me all of the way to Ferndale. You don't recall that?'

'No, I don't.' Hartman rubbed his brow with his right hand. 'It's as odd as hell, isn't it? Pieces have been taken out that should be left in.'

'Then it's all intentional, Frank,' Butch said throatily. 'The crash was laid on to wipe some things from your memory. The things that were connected with Alfred Jones. You figured he might be an alien from outer space. Then he must be, Frank! Don't you see, it all adds up. My wife and the baby. The baby was a girl, Frank, but it was born dead. And you know what Mona told me? There were three other cases identical to hers in the hospital . . . '

He stopped speaking abruptly, seeing that he was making little if any impression on the detective. His mouth had gone slack and he was eyeing Butch queerly.

'A man from outer space! You can't be serious, Butch? And these babies that were stillborn . . . I can't grasp the point. I can't see any significance.'

'You can't see any significance in the fact that you crashed in our street even though there was no other car in your path? You've been told of the tests they did, I'm sure?'

'Yes, I have.' Hartman's cigarette, forgotten, had gone out and he flicked his lighter once more to re-light it. 'It's got the boys baffled, I hear. The doctors in the hospital have put me through the mill to try and sort me out. But now they've given up, I think. They believe that my memory will come back of its own accord. But by then it might be too late, huh?'

'It might be too late, Frank,' was Butch's stony rejoinder.

Butch rose from the chair and gave the detective a weak grin. He said he would see Hartman again when he was up and about.

'It won't be long, Butch. I guess I'll be on my feet in a day or so. What'll bug me most of all is this cracked collarbone. It'll be a few weeks before the bone knits up . . . Butch, there's no reason why you shouldn't tell everything to Jud out there. I — '

'Forget it,' Butch interrupted him, his features grim. 'Jud might drive into our street and crash, and then we'd be back to square one again. So-long, Frank. Next visit I might bring you roses.'

He was at the door when a shrill cry from Frank Hartman stopped him, making the blood congeal in his veins.

'Wait a minute, Butch! Roses, you said. Roses! You took roses to your wife in hospital, didn't you . . . '

It was enough to put Butch swinging about and hurrying over to the detective's bed. Sweat oozed to his brow.

'Yes, roses, Frank. You remember? Then your memory is coming back. Think, Frank, think! Yes, I brought the roses to Mona at the County. They made her ill, and then they withered into nothing. You remember coming to our house? You remember talking with me. About Alfred Jones. About the empty house that wasn't really empty. The room I saw with the strange instrument panels that bleeped and clicked . . . '

'Hell, yes!' Hartman ejaculated. 'It's all coming back to me. Your wife, Mona . . . The baby . . . But you say she didn't have the baby, Butch. It died . . . '

'It was born dead,' Butch answered him vibrantly. 'The same thing happened to three other babies at the hospital. It all adds up, Frank. It must add up. Jones is some kind of weirdo from another planet, like you said. You remember how you left me and got into your car. You drove down the street. There was a crash that brought everybody on the run. It happened opposite the driveway to Jones' house. I hauled you out of the car and we got an ambulance for you. You were taking the box of candies to have them analysed — '

'The candies!' Hartman gulped. He was half-way out of the bed by this time, hardly knowing what he was doing in his agitation. 'Yeah, I took the candies. They were in the car. I crashed . . . No, I didn't crash. There was nothing on the road, Butch. I'll swear to it. Nothing. One minute I was driving along, and then — bam! It was the last thing I knew.'

'Jones must have done it, Frank. It would be easy for him when he can do so much, when he has done so much. He knew who you were and why you were visiting. He knows I must have cottoned on to him. It means he was scared. So he's not above fear after all. His plan isn't as foolproof as he figures it is . . . '

'Yes, yes,' Hartman panted. 'You're right. And the baby was born dead? Other babies at the County were born dead? It's fantastic, Butch. Too fantastic for anyone to swallow. Look, you didn't tell anyone else about this? But no, you said you didn't. Keep your mouth shut, Butch. Don't let Jones know we suspect him. Have you seen him lately?'

'Not since your accident. He claimed to see another car on the road, although everybody else said there was no other car. Here, take it easy,' he added concernedly as Hartman tried to get to his feet. He winced and groaned and sat down on the edge of the bed. He swore in frustration. 'Take it easy,' Butch repeated. 'You're not fit to be moving around yet.'

'The candies, Butch. What happened to the candies?'

Butch explained about the phone call from Jones in relation to the box of candies. Jones said he had seen the box on the street and lifted it. As he talked it occurred to Butch that perhaps the time was ripe for the police to swoop on number twenty and take Alfred Jones into custody.

'No,' Hartman objected. 'What evidence is there against him, Butch? Real evidence, that is? We've nothing to go on but your story. Oh, yes, the car crash is something that has the boys wondering. But you couldn't arrest Jones on the charge of having manipulated it. The case would be laughed out of court. No, Butch, we must be patient for a while longer. We've got to get all the dope we can on him. Jones mightn't be the only alien operating this business.'

'Yeah, you're right,' Butch croaked, appalled at the idea of more than one Jones being abroad. 'But — but what can I do to stop him?'

'You simply string along with him,' Hartman advised. He had crawled back into the bed and was holding his side where his ribs hurt. 'Look at it this way, Butch. Why did Jones latch on to you in the first place?'

'To — to get at my wife,' Butch answered after a short pause. 'Why else?'

'There might be another reason,' the detective suggested. 'If he can do what we think he's done he doesn't need much help from anyone. He said something about you being in favour of making the world a better place for babies, right?'

'Yeah, he did, Frank. You — you don't think he intends to win me over to his cause? But, hell, that's too ridiculous to entertain, isn't it?'

'Maybe it is, Butch. Maybe it's not. How is your wife, by the way?'

Butch told him how Mona seemed to have emerged from the experience with less scars than he bore. They would be discharging her from the County in a few more days.

'That's swell, Butch. All right, then. Do what I ask you to do. Ride along with this character. See where it gets you. See what you can discover about him and his methods. I know it's a pretty tough thing to urge you to do, but pretend to be in sympathy with him and his ideas. If he inquires about me and whether I've regained my memory, tell him a lie. Say I can remember nothing. Don't worry about my colleagues and the police. I'll fix it up with them. Can you do it, pal?'

'I'll try, pal,' Butch agreed with a feeble smile puckering his lips. 'But at the minute it seems that Jones is ignoring me. He didn't even come to offer his sympathy the way some other neighbours did.'

'Then he might not be a complete hypocrite,' Hartman declared with grim humour. 'But my bet says you'll be hearing from him soon. One other thing, Butch: if you catch on that Jones is leaving your street let me know at once. If you want to talk to me for any reason ring the hospital. Get that, Butch?'

'Yeah, I get it. He might pull out of town when he considers his job's done?'

'He might. But I'm hoping he'll want to have a fresh recruit in town before he does leave.'

Butch's heart skipped a beat, but he made a big effort to steady his nerve and resolve.

'I'll feel better when you're able to get around, Frank.'

'Don't worry. If I'm not out of this bed tomorrow my name isn't Frank Hartman.'

Butch left him on that note. Outside the door he was submitted to a searching stare from Jud Holbrook.

'You guys must have had a ball in there,' he observed wryly. 'Any luck with Frank, Deely?'

'Frank can put you in the picture himself,' Butch said shortly and went along the corridor to the elevator.

In the bright sunshine he paused to bring his handkerchief from his pocket to mop his brow. It really was getting warmer by the minute, he thought. But at least it was better than having your spinal column packed in ice. Hartman's recovery of his memory had taken a load from his shoulders. Now he had a friend again, a sincere and helpful sympathizer. If Alfred Jones had a lot of strings hanging at his disposal the same thing could be said for the F.B.I. man.

Only, how did you trap someone if he wasn't human?

Butch went to his car and slid behind the wheel. Before starting the motor running he fingered a cigarette to his lips and got it burning. At this juncture he knew a reluctance to return to Willow Road and his home there. He felt a premonition weighing on him. Supposing it were true that Alfred Jones really did wish to recruit him into his organization, whatever that consisted of? How could he set himself to pretending to go along with Jones when every fibre of his being cried out against the man and his sinister machinations?

As far as he was concerned, Jones — if he actually was responsible for Mona's failure to produce a live baby — had done his worst on him, and therefore he could forget all about the man and that mysterious house he lived in.

'But what about the other expectant mothers in the country?' he gritted in a fit of anger. 'Are you going to let him carry on with his devilish plot?'

Willing or not, it appeared that he was committed to the course advised by the F.B.I. man. Jones took him for a malleable weakling whom he could shape as he wished. Therefore, as a responsible person and citizen, he was obliged to do everything in his power to frustrate his ambitions.

Before going on to Willow Road, Butch stopped off at a bar to drink a beer. He remembered that there was no beer in the house and bought a carton to bring home with him as well. It was drawing on to noon by the time he turned the corner of the street at the north end and proceeded to the driveway leading to his house.

He parked and alighted, slammed the car door and brought his key from his pocket to let himself in.

'Ah, there you are, Butch!'

He swung round abruptly to see Alfred

Jones smiling benignly at him.

Today he wore a neat brown suit that was cut to perfection. He had a white shirt on and a narrow, conservative necktie. The blue eyes glinted behind the spectacle lenses. There was a jaunty air of confidence about him that tended to belie the mildness in his eyes.

'Oh, hello, Alfred,' Butch greeted him in a tone that was as firm as he could make it. For a fleeting instant he could see himself walking over to the man and landing a full-blooded punch to the point of his chin. How would Jones react if he did this? Would he wilt under pressure and ultimately confess to the devilish influence he was capable of exerting?

'Why, what's the matter, Butch? Oh, I'd almost forgotten. Your dear lady wife. The baby . . .'

'The baby didn't live, Alfred.'

'Yes, I know. Such a tragedy, Butch. Such an awful tragedy! And how is your wife keeping, may I ask?'

'She's okay,' Butch answered shortly. He yielded to a mood that was coloured with recklessness. 'I've got a few beers here. Won't you come in and drink one?'

'Thank you, Butch,' Jones said, his smile widening. 'I'll be happy to accept your invitation. Although, to tell you the truth, I intended hunting you up with the intention of extending an invitation of my own.'

'Oh,' Butch murmured with his heart jolting against his ribs. 'What kind of invitation?'

'To visit me at my house, Butch. Remember how I said I'd like the opportunity to have another chat with you, a long undisturbed chat concerning aspects of things we might have in common?'

'Yes, I do remember. But I've been busy . . . ' He inserted the key in the lock and opened the door. He stood aside and gestured for Jones to go into the house in front of him. Jones inclined his head slightly and entered.

In the living-room he turned to Butch, removing his spectacles and exposing small blue eyes that glittered with the intensity of laser beams.

'Stand right where you are, Butch, and listen to me,' he ordered softly.

15

The small eyes seemed to widen, to attain depth, and Butch Deely had the sensation of being poised on the brink of a deep blue lake that was wonderfully attractive and inviting. His resentment towards Alfred Jones melted and fell away from him. He saw Jones — not as a menace to him and Mona or to anybody else — but as a friend who was standing ready and waiting to lend what advice and assistance that might be called for.

The very room where they stood lost substance and dimension, and now Butch saw a vista of meadows and hills, of gleaming silver streams and rivers that spread as far as the eye could see under a blue sky. He had never seen anything like it anywhere.

Butch wanted to shake himself, to retain some firm hold on reality and not let go. But he didn't have the strength — or perhaps he lacked the will — to challenge the validity of this marvellous vision.

It would be so easy to let go, to relinquish everything that life had meant for him so far, and give up his thoughts and his senses to the adoration of this representation of perfection.

Alfred Jones' voice ran across the vibrating surface of his consciousness.

'Butch . . . Do you hear me, Butch?'

'Yes, I hear you, Mr Jones.'

'There is no need to call me *Mr* Jones, Butch. We are firm friends, so let's be free and informal with each other.'

'Just as you say, Alfred.'

'You mentioned something about a beer, my dear boy.'

'Beer?' Butch echoed in a tone that he scarcely recognized as his own. 'I don't want beer, Alfred.'

'Why do you not want beer, Butch? Are you not thirsty any longer?'

'No. I'm not thirsty.'

'But you are still a trifle frightened, Butch. That is so, isn't it?'

'Frightened?' The word came tentatively from his lips, as if it was one he had difficulty in plumbing and comprehending. 'No, I don't think I am frightened.'

'But you were frightened, Butch. Apprehensive.'

'Yes, I suppose that I was.'

'What were you frightened of? Whom were you frightened of?'

'I — I don't know. I'm not sure . . . ' He was reluctant to talk at this juncture. Words fell like unwieldy rocks into the smoothness of the vision. The tops of the hills rippled a little. The water running in the rivers and streams became turbid. Even the blue sky trembled under the disturbance — the way a TV picture rippled in agitation if someone opened up with an unsuppressed motorized lawnmower. In another way, it was similar to a state where you were dropping off to sleep and someone kept nudging you to keep you awake.

'You were frightened of me, Butch.'

'No,' he protested with feeling. 'No.'

'It is unnecessary to withhold the truth, Butch. The truth won't hurt me, you understand. Do tell the truth, Butch. You were frightened of me?'

Butch heard himself laughing; it sounded like disembodied, uncontrolled merriment.

'That was stupid of me, Alfred. Do you know, the thought even crossed my mind that I wanted to kill you.'

'Because of what?' the soft voice prodded. 'Because of the roses? They were beautiful roses, though. Can you see where they come from, Butch?'

'Yes, yes, I think I do, Alfred. I see a cluster of them waving in the breeze.'

'What else do you see?'

'Hills, green fields — meadows. Streams. But, Alfred, there is something missing.'

'What is missing?' Jones said to him, his tone roughened by the faintest trace of annoyance.

'Birds, Alfred. There are no birds . . . But that's a ridiculous thing to say, isn't it? This is happening nowhere but in my mind. It's just a dream, isn't it? You wanted me to see something that would calm me?'

'You are seeing Ger, my dear boy. But just a small portion of the land, of course.'

'Ger! Where is Ger?'

'It is a land of perfection,' Jones said gently. 'You humans crave after perfection, don't you? But you crave after you know not what. You have never seen perfection because the world you live in is an imperfect world. But one day your world will emulate ours, Butch. I am here to teach you, to show you the folly of your ways. To show you that it is wrong to bring children into an imperfect world. The children seek for perfection from the first moment they draw a breath. But what do they find? They grow up to discord and disillusionment. They see a pattern of living that is wrong, but they have not the ability to discriminate. Before you can discriminate you must have points of relation. Do you understand that, Butch?'

'Yes . . . I believe I see what you're driving at, Alfred. Alfred! The picture is fading. It's going away . . .'

'Then listen,' Jones said urgently. 'Do exactly as I say, Butch. Forget all of this for the present. Erase it from your conscious thinking, but file it away, nevertheless, in the depths of your memory so that you can refer to it when the occasion to do so arises. Do you understand me, Butch?'

'Yes, I do.' Butch's voice was thickening. It came to his own ears like an amplified, delayed echo.

'Good. You will come to my house tonight, Butch. At ten o'clock sharp, mind you. You will be there, Butch?'

'I'll be there, Alfred. But what — '

'No more questions now. All will be made clear to you in due course.'

Butch shook his head and looked at Jones.

He saw the mild blue eyes through the spectacle lenses. There was a hint of question in the eyes that he found baffling.

'What is it, Alfred? Did you say something?'

'Yes, I said I'd be glad to have a beer. The weather really is getting hot, isn't it. Shall I open the beers for you?'

'No, let me do it.'

He carried the carton into the kitchen and Alfred Jones followed him. He marvelled at the neatness of everything. The refrigerator was a new one, was it not?

'Yeah, you're right,' Butch told him. 'It is. We bought it new not more than three months ago. The old one was giving too much trouble, you see. So we decided to hand it in in a part-exchange deal . . . '

He had the feeling that he wanted to go on talking to Jones. The man seemed to be curious about so much, and the interest he evinced had an attractive quality that was almost naïve.

'What kind of fridge do you have, Alfred?'

'It's a trifle out-dated, I'm afraid,' the other chuckled, taking the can of beer and the extended glass. 'Where shall we sit, Butch? Here or in the living-room?'

'Anwhere you like, Alfred.'

'Then I'll sit here,' Jones smiled and perched himself on a stool beside the stove. It was the stool that Mona used when she wanted to park herself by something special she was cooking for dinner.

Butch's eyes hardened momentarily as

he regarded the immaculate figure. Jones sipped the beer like wine instead of consuming it in healthy mouthfuls. The sunlight coming through the window glanced off the spectacle lenses when he lifted his head. He saw the tail end of Butch's expression and paused in his sipping.

'What is it, Butch? Something is troubling you? You looked extremely angry for a moment then.'

'Did I?' Butch shrugged and wondered at the twinge of guilt he felt. 'What is there to be angry about?'

'Oh, I can't answer that, my dear boy. But you have been subjected to a lot of worry lately . . . '

'Yeah, I have,' Butch grunted. He swallowed off the beer and flung the can at the trash bin. He immediately proceeded to open another can.

'Do you drink a lot, Butch?'

'No, not a lot. But what's a couple of beers? They never hurt anyone, did they?' He realized that for some reason he wanted to whip himself into a temper. He had the strangest feeling that the mild man sitting in front of him was possessed with a secret knowledge that would be distasteful and upsetting were he to be inclined to divulge it.

It was queer. Very queer. For a little while — on entering the house — he had known a confusion. His thoughts had become jumbled and incoherent. He wondered why. He wondered if Alfred Jones had been in any way responsible. And why had he invited Jones into his house to sit there, smug and confident, on Mona's stool? Yes, he was smug and confident behind that gentle, diffident exterior. But why had he come here? What did he wish to talk about? Hartman?

A chill streaked to Butch's groin and fastened there. He drank the beer straight from the can, then flung the empty at the trash bin. Jones appeared unruffled and in complete command of himself. He reminded Butch of a tolerant parent awaiting the evaporation of a sulky mood from a spoiled child.

He essayed a weak laugh.

'You know, Alfred, I'm trying to figure

out why you came to see me like this. Did you have something on your mind?'

Jones smiled and laid his beer glass aside. He had drunk only about half the quantity Butch had given him. He brought a white handkerchief from his pocket and wiped his hands. He did this delicately, like a fastidious person adhering to ingrained habit.

'I merely came to offer my sympathy to you, Butch. But I dare say you have business to attend to and I have overstayed my welcome.'

'No, of course you haven't,' Butch objected quickly as he came off the stool and moved to the kitchen doorway. 'I like someone around to talk to now and again. I — '

'All the same, I'd better be going, Butch.' He reached the doorway and halted to look back at the other. 'Oh, yes, it has just occurred to me to ask you about the gentleman who was injured in the car crash. Have you heard anything of him at all?'

' — uh — No, I haven't . . . But yes, I have. What I mean is, I phoned the

hospital to ask about him. He's progress-
ing well, they told me. He should be able
to get around in a day or so.'

'Splendid! I'm so glad to hear it. And
his memory, Butch? Did they intimate
whether Mr Hartman had recovered his
memory?'

'It seems that he hasn't,' Butch said
from dry lips.

'Indeed! You are certainly having your
share of misfortune, Butch. But the tide
will turn, never fear. You said that Mr
Hartman was a friend of the family,
Butch. On your side or on your wife's
side?'

'Hey, wait a minute, Alfred. He isn't a
relation. Just an old acquaintance.'

'Of course. And I've no right to be
prying. Well, I'll leave you with my best
wishes. Perhaps I'll see you again soon.'

'Yeah, you might at that, Alfred.'

He accompanied Jones to the front
door and saw him out. The sun shone
brightly from a cloudless sky and yet
there seemed to be a decided chill in the
air for all that. As Butch watched Alfred
Jones walk down the driveway he yielded

to a sudden, inexplicable impulse.

'Alfred — Mr Jones . . . Wait!'

Jones wheeled and regarded him steadily. A slight breeze lifted a strand of his hair and blew it up under the brim of the hat he had drawn on when he emerged.

'What is it, Butch?'

'Must you really go so soon? I'm sorry if I appeared to be inhospitable. You see, I — '

'I understand, Butch. I understand perfectly. But you misrepresent yourself, I'm afraid. You have not been inhospitable. You must not imagine that you have.'

'Then — then I'll see you later?'

'I'm looking forward to it, Butch. Good-bye for now.'

He was gone from Butch's view.

Butch was sweating as he turned back into the house. The house seemed more empty than ever now, he thought. More forlorn, more desolate. Whatever Jones was, he radiated an extremely potent force. An attraction.

'Hell, what am I thinking!' Butch cried

in an outburst of total confusion. 'What's going on? First off I want to get him by the neck and throttle the life out of him. Now I want him to hang around and smile at me through those goddam glasses! What gives? Am I really flipping under the pressure?'

He had a need to see Mona just then, a need to talk to her and confide in her. He would put her in the picture concerning the latest events.

The latest events! Who was he kidding? He hadn't even brought Mona up to date as it was. He had been determined to drop the subject of Jones as far as she was concerned. She knew nothing about his visits to that house, about the cops calling, or Frank Hartman calling. Was he prepared to submit his wife to a new array of worries and fears?

'No, I can't do it,' he choked. 'Mona has come through enough as it is. She's okay at the minute, but reaction might set in. It's almost certain to set in when she comes home from the hospital . . . '

The burring of the phone sent him

lunging towards it. He gripped the hand-piece in unsteady fingers and announced himself. It was a call from the County, likely. Mona was ill. She was — '

'Hello, Butch,' Frank Hartman's voice jarred in his ear. 'Look, I've been reading several out-of-town papers. I got this notion, you see, after you left me. Butch, you know that the closest town to Caldwell is Oakville . . . '

'Sure I know,' Butch said from a constricted throat. 'You've got an Oakville paper? What about it?'

'Just this,' the detective went on excitedly. 'There was an item in the paper — just a few paragraphs stuck away in the centre pages. Well, they've taken up the Courier feature and are making comparisons. We really are on to something, fella. The birth rate in Oakville has been falling steadily over the past six months. Judging by the tone of the article they're not in a serious frame of mind about it. Not yet, that is. The stupes can't work it out for themselves that something is radically wrong.'

'I see,' Butch said in a taut whisper. 'So

it's starting to happen in Oakville as well. But you can't blame Alfred Jones for that, Frank.'

'I can't blame him for what? What's the matter with you, Butch? You're not trying to give this guy Jones a clean bill of health in the light of what we know about him?'

'What do we know, Frank?'

'Hey, slow down, Deely! What's come over you? You're telling me you're getting a change of heart?'

'I don't understand you, Frank.'

'I damn-well don't understand you, mister.' There was a tense pause and then Frank Hartman continued. 'Tell me, something, Butch,' he said with a new inflexion. 'Have you run across this guy Jones since you saw me here?'

'Yeah, I have.'

'What — what did you talk about? What did he say to you? Did he say anything to you?'

'Nothing out of the ordinary. He just came visiting. He wanted to say he was sorry about the baby — '

'The double-talking bastard! But no,

275

Butch. Wait a minute. I'm simply running on, you see. But I'm hooked good and solid on this gag. The more I think of it the more I'm convinced that Jones is not what he seems to be. He's not a man at all, Butch!'

'Oh,' Butch said, rubbing his forehead where a steel band appeared to be pressing. 'I — I — don't follow you, Frank. I'm feeling kind of tired of all this guessing. I'd like to slow down for a day or so. Get my bearings.'

Again that tense silence. When Hartman spoke once more his tone was taut with the control he was exerting.

'Something is happening, Butch. To you, boy. Do you get what I'm attempting to put over?'

'Yes, I think so.'

'Good. Then take a grip on yourself. Hold on, Butch. You've simply got to hold on. For your own sake. For your wife's sake. For the sake of everyone else in this country. Did you bring Jones into the house when he visited?'

'Yeah, I did. Why not? I couldn't keep him standing on the doorstep.'

'What did you do? What did you say? You didn't tell him how my memory was okay?'

'I didn't, Frank. I just gave him a beer. We talked in the kitchen for a short time. About nothing in particular.'

'He didn't try selling you anything? Remember, Butch, he picked on you for a purpose. Don't forget it. Be on your guard. Did he try selling you a line?'

'No, he didn't. Why should he? I'm no chump, Frank.'

'I hope you're not,' Hartman rejoined weightily. 'All right then, Butch. Like I said, hold on. See as little of this guy as you can. Avoid him if possible until I'm able to get around. It won't be long, I promise you. By tomorrow they might let me out of this damned bed. Okay, Butch?'

'Okay, Frank. Good-bye.'

That evening he drove to the County Hospital as usual, and was gratified to find Mona in good spirits. But she remarked on his paleness and his air of abstraction, using her own terms to describe this. What he needed was a short break, free from worry. How did the notion of an early holiday up in the woods appeal to him? He enjoyed living in one of those chalets, where he could fish and hunt to his heart's content. She could do with a break as well.

'Sure,' he said, smiling at her. 'It's a date, sweetie. I'll organize it the minute you're back home.'

He left the hospital at nine-thirty with a vague thought nagging steadily at him. There was something he wanted to do tonight. What was it he wanted to do tonight? Yes, now he had it. Alfred Jones. He wished to see Jones again. He wished to have another look at the house where he lived. Hartman had told him to cultivate Jones, hadn't he? Well then, he would cultivate.

He drove home and parked his car on the driveway. In the house he had a shower and drank a bottle of beer. By then it was drawing on to ten. He had certainly lost no time since leaving the hospital. With a cigarette at the corner of his mouth, he strode through the shadows thronging the street to reach number twenty.

The door opened to his first pressure on the bell button.

Jones smiled at him and invited him inside.

16

Butch had the feeling now of following the clearly defined outlines of a pattern. So long as he kept to the guiding lines everything would be all right: there would be no reason for him to pause and consider, nor to spend any time in examining his conscience. It appeared that all that had been taken into account and disposed of. By entering this house he was entering another plane of living, another level of consciousness.

Leading him on — like a carrot dangling a few inches from a donkey's nose — was the promise of another view of that wonderful land where everything was created to perfection. Strange how this notion had implanted itself in his brain on the moment he crossed the threshold of number twenty! Or was it so strange? Perhaps he had been going around, intellectually blind, for years, and only now had true wisdom decided to favour him.

Naturally, Butch Deely reflected in his own terms, but, in effect, this was what he was thinking.

Alfred Jones kept glancing over his shoulder as he led Butch into the living-room. The furnishings and decor registered comfortably with the memory of his other visit in company with the two police officers. Jones' smile widened and became a beam that transformed his face.

He was not just a mild, gentle-looking creature at this stage; he was a man who had pulled off a remarkable feat of which he was extremely proud. Butch didn't mind him being proud. He had always believed that a man had the right to display whatever he felt, whether it be anger, disappointment, joy or triumph. Yes, that word described the aura surrounding Jones exactly. He exuded triumph. He was pleased with himself and he was willing to embrace Butch Deely in his pleasure.

'My dear Butch, I am so glad that you came. Do you know, Butch, that, up to the very last moment, I could not say definitely whether you would come. Perhaps you might call it a calculated risk — to use well-worn coinage. Perhaps you would simply call it a gamble and let it go at that. But I dare say you hardly know what I'm talking about,' Jones appended with a sharp little chuckle.

He gestured to a lounging chair and Butch sank down obediently. Automatically he fingered for his cigarettes, produced a pack and slid one from the pack to his lips. He had mislaid his lighter, but he had a folder of paper matches and he used one of these to ignite the cigarette tip. He puffed and gazed around him.

Suddenly his eyes touched a candy box on the table and his reflexes froze momentarily.

'What — what's that?' he asked hoarsely when he had found his voice. 'Where did you get it?'

'Candies, Butch. The box I purchased for your wife. At least, I think it is the same box. Would you care to try one of the candies, Butch?'

'No, no,' he said quickly, shaking his head. 'I don't want any candies, Alfred.'

'Why? Don't you like candies?'

'They're okay. I fancy them now and again. Not often.'

'I see. And of course you would be reluctant to sample something which you believed to be tampered with.'

'Tampered with? I don't get it, Alfred.'

'Oh, come, come, my dear fellow. You get it well enough. Why did you not present them to your wife, Butch?' He had eased himself on to a chair opposite Butch and the room lighting reflected on the spectacle lenses. With a swift motion he took the spectacles from the bridge of his nose, exposing the small blue eyes.

They drilled into Butch.

'Mona . . . didn't like them,' he heard himself panting.

'Then she tried them? She sampled them?'

'Yes . . . Yeah, she did.'

'But there are none missing from the box,' Jones reminded him with a trace of irritation in his tone. 'There is no reason to lie to me, Butch. No reason at all.

Unless we can be absolutely frank with each other, then I'm afraid we cannot proceed.'

'Proceed? Where to, Alfred?'

'To Ger, eventually. The land of perfection, Butch. You have often dreamed of such a land, I'm sure. It is the little island within every man's heart. But it can be more than a dream, Butch. It *is* more than a dream. But to get there a man must be honest and sincere in everything he says and does. Would you claim to be honest and sincere, Butch?'

'I — I could try, I guess. Couldn't I?' he added eagerly. 'You could show me how to try?'

'I can show you, my dear fellow.' Jones indulged in another, softer, chuckle. He indicated the box of candies. 'You did not offer them to your wife?'

'No, I didn't.'

'You thought they might be poisoned? Your wife was upset by the roses and you didn't wish to upset her with the candies?'

'Yeah, that's right. I bought her another box of candies. She ate one and I ate one.

But she found she didn't care for those, either.'

'You needn't have worried, Butch. The roses nor the candies would not have harmed your wife. Presenting them to you was merely a variation which I was experimenting with.' He threw his head back and gave a short laugh. Somehow or other he had replaced his spectacles without Butch having noticed that he did.

'What's so funny, Alfred?'

'Something occurred to me that amuses me. You might understand and you might not. But in a way you represent my biggest success to date. I have disproved the fallacy that the most intelligent people are the easiest to disorientate and manipulate subsequently. You were a challenge to me, Butch. Not just you as an individual, you understand, but the stratum of society which you symbolize. Who could be more hard-headed and down to earth than a driver of a truck? I have three scientists in my book. Four doctors — or perhaps it is five doctors. Two are medical men and the others can boast of degrees in psychology and philosophy. There are two school-teachers, also, a couple of — '

'What has that got to do with it, Alfred? I simply don't get you. Why are they in your book? What do they do?'

'They are my disciples, Butch, my adherents. I will not insult the gentlemen by referring to them as minions. But all of them have one golden gift in common — the promise of ultimate sanctuary and happiness on the planet Ger.'

'You decided to recruit me as well?'

'Recruit?' Jones toyed with the word for a few seconds. He nodded, smiling. 'Recruit, perhaps. Friend, most definitely. But there is work to be done, and I have to ask whether you would be willing to undertake that work.'

'Doing what, Alfred?'

'You would be an agent, Butch. One of my growing band of agents. After a suitable number of instruction sessions you would move away from Caldwell. You would take your wife with you, of course. Your wife does not have to know what you're doing.'

'What would I be doing?'

'Helping with my work, Butch. Helping your world and the people in it to discover their errors, their failures. Your planet has been chosen for the initial experiment. The plan is divided into stages, and the first step in the plan is to call a halt to the birth of new babies. At the present my other agents are active in this field. You will be taught how to emulate their efforts. You will leave Caldwell, as I say, Butch, and go to another town of my choosing. Once there you will drop Deely and change your name to Jones. Your task will be of a full-time nature, but you won't have to worry about earning money to live. You will be paid a salary, Butch. You will be happy at your work. Your wife will be happy and agreeable . . . '

'My wife . . . Mona likes things as they are, Alfred. She intends to have a baby — '

'It's out of the question, Butch,' Jones interrupted him sharply. 'You, of all people, must set a worthy example. I said it was wrong to bring children into an imperfect world and it is. Bringing birth itself to a halt is only the first step on the way. The next stage will entail social surgery on a large scale . . . '

'Social surgery?'

'It's merely a term, Butch. You humans communicate in spoken language. You think in word symbols. On Ger you simply think and your thoughts are transmitted at will. Words as such build more barriers than they destroy. You use them as shields for your thoughts and as weapons for your emotions . . . To return to the subject, Butch. When birth has been halted the next step is to carve out other imperfections. Evil, insanity, deformity of body and of mind . . . '

'You — you'd kill off the people who are unwell, unhealthy? The people who are mentally unbalanced?'

'There is no reason to sound shocked, my dear fellow. It is all a matter of perspective. Your perspective has been shaped by this earthly civilization, and therein lies the chief fault. But it will be remedied, and ultimately pure logic will prevail.'

'No,' Butch whispered, some fibre of his consciousness stirring and revolting. 'No, Alfred, you can't do it. I won't let you do it. I'll tell Frank. I'll tell him everything.'

'Your friend from the federal department?' Jones' smile was tolerant, indulgent. With what appeared to be a casual movement he lifted off his spectacles once more. The small blue eyes widened to engulf Butch, to absorb him and his thoughts and his very identity. He glimpsed those green fields again, those rolling hills, the silver-crested rivers and streams. And he heard birdsong that held him enraptured.

'Beautiful, Alfred! Wonderful!'

'To attain it you must do what I say, Butch. Do you hear me, my friend, my good friend? Are you ready to heed me?'

'I hear you, Alfred. I'll heed you.'

'Splendid! Your so-called friend from the Federal Bureau of Investigation recovered his memory, did he not?'

'Yes, he did.'

'You talked to him at length, Butch? You told him all that you had experienced?'

'Yes, I did. He crashed his car, you see. But they're sure he didn't strike another car on the street. How did he crash?'

'He struck an invisible obstruction, Butch. A force field of my contriving.'

'The branch on my tree was broken, Alfred. I couldn't understand how it happened.'

'It happened, Butch. It was a symbolic gesture to my people back home on Ger. While I'm here they have contact with me and your world. Were I to leave, that contact would be broken. There is only one way that I and my system can be eradicated, Butch. I took over this house and endowed it with qualities which we take for granted on Ger, but which, in practice, seem alien and fantastic to ordinary human intellectual perception.'

'How, Alfred?'

'You want to get to Ger, Butch? It is your aim now, the pinnacle of all your aspirations?'

'I want to get to Ger. I must get to Ger . . .'

'Irrespective of other considerations? All other considerations? Answer me truthfully, Butch.'

'Nothing else matters, Alfred.'

'Your wife?'

'My wife is strong and healthy. She can fend for herself.'

'And your ambition to have children?'

'It is wrong to have children. The world is not a proper place for children. One day it may be ready for children.'

'Fire, my dear fellow.'

'Fire?' Butch muttered, feeling himself in a haze that insulated him from his previous conception of reality. Suddenly he felt frightened of fire. Whatever happened, he must stay away from fire.

'That is it, Butch. Once you become a true agent you must reject and abhor fire. Fire can destroy. It is unknown on Ger and we have not learned how to combat it. Benevolent heat is another thing entirely, of course. Fire can destroy you. Fire can destroy this building. Fire is the most destructive force there is.'

'I understand you, Alfred.'

'Are you ready then, Butch?'

'Ready? For what?'

'To be introduced to my people. I have

been in touch with them tonight and a representative panel is awaiting the introduction procedure.'

'I'm . . . frightened, Alfred.'

'You need not be frightened. You need not be alarmed. Please get up now, Butch, and come with me.'

Butch rose, much as an automaton would react to a control switch. He followed Alfred Jones out of the living-room and into the kitchen at the rear. Now memory contrived a positive mael-strom of conflicting anxieties and desires. One part of him was eager and ready to go anywhere with Jones; another part of him shuddered in a paroxysm of revolt.

'Do come along, Butch. There is nothing to worry about.'

Jones had his hand on the knob of the kitchen door now. He pushed the door open and the secret chamber was visible to Butch's eyes once more. There was the row of instrument panels, winking and fluttering to the accompaniment of those strange clickings and tappings. There were two chairs arranged in front of a large, dark screen. Jones seated himself on one of the chairs and motioned for Butch to sit beside him on the other.

As soon as Butch sank down Jones reached across and pressed a small button below the screen.

'You may be surprised, my dear fellow. You may even be amazed at what you see. But, as I say, there is nothing to worry about. Perfection is oneness with your neighbours and the universe. Where there are no opposing factions there can be no friction. Therein lies the key to the ultimate truth.'

The screen glowed and blurred. A picture came vaguely and retreated before steadying and brightening. Butch uttered a sharp cry and almost fell off his chair. Jones gripped his arm and held him until the shock passed. His eyes glued to the screen.

He saw four men seated at a round table. They seemed to be in a large room that had a high, domed ceiling through which a snatch of brilliant blue sky was visible. But the remarkable thing about these men was that they were all identical with Alfred Jones, minus his spectacles.

Not a shade of difference could Butch see in the physical make-up, in the way the small blue eyes stabbed out of the screen at him.

'Who are they, Alfred?' he heard himself croaking. 'They all look like you. Are they your brothers?'

'It is precisely what they are, Butch,' Jones answered in a soft voice without taking his attention from the screen. 'My brothers. But not brothers in the sense that you conceive and understand. On Ger every man is a brother to his fellow. Every woman is a sister. It is what I meant by saying perfection is oneness with your neighbours. Please be silent while I communicate with them.'

Butch watched, utterly fascinated, while the eyes of the men seemed to lock with Jones'. No word was spoken, no physical gesture was made. At the end of, perhaps, five minutes, Jones turned his head to Butch and smiled at him.

'They are in complete agreement with my choice, Butch. They welcome you to the brotherhood of Ger. But they are insistent on one very important aspect of this relationship. It must be a secret one for the present. You must be willing and ready to obey me to the letter. You appreciate that, don't you?'

'Yes, I do, Alfred.'

Jones concentrated on the screen for another few minutes. Then he raised his hand, palm outwards and the four men at the table did likewise.

'Give the salute, Butch.'

Butch raised his right hand, also, imitating the salute to the men on Ger. Jones stretched over to the switch and pressed the button twice in quick succession. The screen went blank.

Jones signalled that he should rise and they left the room together. Now Jones faced the room through the kitchen door and raised his head slightly. He stood with his eyes closed, and Butch watched in astonishment while the secret chamber disintegrated in a soft, smoke-like cloud.

There was the back yard of the house, with its weeds and the discarded plastic bucket and spade. Aloft, the stars scintillated in the velvet heavens. A light breeze whispered across the yard, and in the distance Butch heard the slow, muted passage of an automobile down the street. A shiver took him.

'Watch for the final sign now, Butch.'

Jones pointed to the heavens where only the charted planets stood out against the anonymous stars. Butch stared, waiting for that mysterious star to flare into significant prominence. It did so and his gaze sought it and clung to it. Even when the light could have been termed blinding, as it had been before when he was unable to look at it, he continued to watch the star. A feeling of security and comfort encompassed him, and he had neither the desire nor the will to reject the sensation.

'That is all for now, Butch.'

He went into the living-room of the house with Jones, and there the gently smiling man extended his right hand for Butch to clasp. Butch offered his own hand readily and was amazed at the coldness of those rock-firm fingers.

'Go, man of Ger to be. Whatever happens tomorrow, you must return to this house at ten o'clock. In the meantime, be your usual self, Butch Deely. Good-bye.'

He left Butch to find his own way from the house, and when he passed through the front doorway the door closed after him, making him jerk and pause to regard the façade of the building.

Suddenly that was an empty house once more, curtainless and lifeless. It was as though Alfred Jones had another mission to fulfil tonight and was off in haste to keep some rendezvous.

Butch plodded down the driveway to the street, but halted again on noticing something strange about the front yard. The sign was in place where it had been before. He forced himself to walk over to the sign and read it. 'For Sale'. No 'Sold' cancellation sticker. Butch retreated and continued to the street. He walked back to his own house like a man forever lost in the depths of a trance.

17

It turned out to be the worst night that Butch Deely had ever experienced. For at least an hour after he returned home he sat in the living-room, looking straight in front of him, seeing nothing but the smiling eyes of Alfred Jones, hearing nothing but the voice of the man from Ger.

'Bringing birth itself to a halt is only the first step on the way. The next stage will entail social surgery on a large scale . . . '

Jones had chosen him to be one of his followers, one of his disciples. After suitable training he would be sent off on a mission of his own. While helping to save mankind from his folly he would be paving a pathway to Ger at the same time. That land of rounded hills, green meadows and silver streams and rivers would be his reward. It should have been called Paradise instead of Ger. And perhaps indeed it was Paradise, for what else could you call a land where perfection reigned?

Finally Butch rolled into bed and slept. Sleeping, he was subjected to the nightmares of the damned. And how could he tell that they were nothing but nightmares?

He saw a procession of children marching along a road that was thick in night shadow. They seemed to be chanting a song, but neither the words nor the music were clear enough to be understood. And there in the forefront of the procession was his wife, Mona. Mona was carrying a banner on which was emblazoned the figure of a child with a scorpion at its throat. He heard clearly enough what his wife was saying.

'Here they are, Butch. All your children. The children you forbade to come on to the earth. Now they are going off and leaving you. They will never come back to you and neither will I. You are the doomed, Butch. We are alive and free.'

He seemed to yell and run after the procession of children, wanting to reach

Mona, to touch her, to ask her to wait until he explained. But the children grasped him and held him and refused to let him reach his wife. And suddenly the words they chanted became perfectly lucid and understandable.

'Butch is the killer. Butch is the killer. Butch tried to keep us from coming alive.'

Again, he was standing at the kitchen door of number twenty and Alfred Jones was commanding him to look on Ger and tell him what he saw there. Butch looked and saw five men sitting at that conference table. All of the five were identical in appearance, and he realized the fifth man was himself. Truly, he had become another Mr Jones.

'I don't want to be Alfred Jones,' he shouted. 'I'm Butch Deely. I want to be who I am. I don't want to be anyone else . . .'

Thus the night hours passed. A night of horror for the ravaged subconscious mind of Butch Deely. When dawn at last stained the sky to the east he opened his eyes and murmured a fervent prayer of gratitude.

Yet he knew he was not free of the chains. He was still shackled, psychologically, to the man who had come to deliver the people of the earth from the folly of their ways.

He struggled into the bathroom and stared at his reflection in the shaving mirror. Once his eyes met their reflection in the glass he averted them quickly. It was a mistake to look at himself. He could not afford to look inwards now. He must keep looking away from himself. If he didn't he might go mad.

The telephone in the living-room burred.

'Mona!' he gasped, lunging to the phone and grabbing up the receiver. 'Butch Deely here! Is that the County — '

'It's me, Butch,' Frank Hartman's flat voice inserted itself. 'I know it's early for ringing, Butch, but how do you feel this morning?'

'I feel fine,' he croaked into the mouthpiece. 'What way do you think I feel? You're nothing but a goddam snoop, Hartman. Well, keep your snooping nose our of my business. Get it?'

'No — wait, Butch! Don't hang up. I'm coming over there to see you. Do you hear me, Butch? You're not feeling well, are you? Something has happened since I saw you last. Jones . . . '

'The hell with Jones!' Butch screamed into the mouthpiece. 'I'm going to find him and tear him to pieces . . . '

He slammed the instrument down on its rest. Then he balled his right fist and drove it at the wall. His shoulders trembled and went into a convulsive heave, and the next moment Butch Deely was on his knees on the floor, crying and blubbering like a terrified baby.

★ ★ ★

He roused when the doorbell buzzed. He rose, dry-eyed and hard of feature. With deliberate steps he entered the hall and went on to open the front door. Frank Hartman stood there, pale and strained looking, his left arm in a sling to favour his broken collarbone. Hartman had a companion with him, this a tall, reedy individual with a cheerful face and small

302

scar under his right eye.

'Hello, Butch,' the detective greeted as he brushed past him and indicated for his companion to do likewise. 'You can see that I made it. You didn't do anything foolish, did you?'

'No, I didn't.' Butch followed them into the living-room and Hartman proceeded to introduce the skinny man.

'This is John Davies, Butch. He's a professor of physics. He — '

'But I thought you intended keeping this to yourself,' Butch protested. 'Now you're going to bring everybody in on the deal. What do I want with a professor?' he added angrily. 'Who needs a professor?'

'Slow down, Butch. I just had to do it. I knew it was necessary to get extra help and I asked for it. This is getting too big for the two of us to handle. Now, Butch,' the detective continued steadily, 'I've given John the picture as far as I know it. But more has happened since we talked, hasn't it? You've seen Jones again. He said something or did something to get you over to his way of thinking. Am I right, Butch?'

For several seconds Butch considered the two men without speaking. Once more a battle raged inside him, opposing forces fighting for possession of his mind, his body, his soul . . .

A hoarse cry emerged from his constricted throat.

'Yes, yes, Frank. Something else happened. If I don't get help soon I'll go crazy. I know I'll go crazy.'

'Take it easy, Mr Deely,' John Davies urged and guided him to a chair. 'Sit down there and tell me all about it.'

* * *

'Fire!' Davies said musingly when he had heard the recital through to the end. 'The old, sure-fire method of cleansing.' His gaze touched the horrified eyes of Frank Hartman. 'It's kind of hard to swallow, Frank, is it not?'

'It's weird without doubt, John. But there's no doubt in my mind that it happened the way Butch said. Jones really has set him up for an agent. And he's got his agents scattered all over the place?

Boy, oh, boy! This book he spoke of, Butch. Any idea where he keeps it?'

'I don't know,' Butch answered in a hollow voice. He saw how close he had come to falling over the edge. One more session with Jones and the man from Ger would have had him hooked. 'Where else would he have it but in that secret room where the signalling and communication apparatus is? But if the room doesn't actually exist . . . '

'The room exists only as a thought,' John Davies declared soberly. 'As a vibration from this planet. As a radio wave-length, if you care to call it that. But it's real enough to Jones, and this book should be real enough to us. He told you to visit at the same time tonight, Butch. Well, here's what you must do. You must go along to number twenty tonight. Pretend that you're well and truly under Jones' spell. Then try and get it out of him where this book is. Once we have the addresses of these agents he has through-out the country we can hit them one by one. I just hope to heaven we can do it, Frank. And I hope it can be done without starting a world-wide panic. Will you do it, Butch? You simply must do it. Get that book somehow and give it to Frank or me.'

'What — what happens if I get the book?' Butch asked him. 'You'll set the house up in smoke? Jones along with it?'

'It's the only way,' Davies declared forcefully. 'Frank, you'll have to take the chief of police into your confidence. Get him to arrange to lay on fire tenders to prevent the whole street going up in flames. It would be advisable to evacuate Jones' immediate neighbours, but it would have to be done discreetly.'

'Yes, I get it, John. As well as that we'll have to arrange some method of keeping in touch with Butch while he's in the house. Butch, you'll do exactly as we tell you?'

'I'll do what I can,' Butch promised with a weak grin. 'But I just hope to hell Jones isn't listening to us now. If he can play around with that house and pop up where he wants to, then he's going to be a tough bird to pin down.'

'We've got to pin him down,' John

Davies said vehemently. 'If this man is allowed to plant enough seeds he can upset the balance of the entire world.'

★　★　★

For the rest of the day Butch endeavoured to behave normally. He made two visits to Mona at the County Hospital and was more relieved than ever at the progress she was making.

'I must be a lot harder than I imagined I was, darling,' she said with a trace of wistfulness in her tone. 'I only hope I won't end up being as tough as an old boot.'

'You'll never be an old boot, sweetie, so put your mind at rest. We're going to have another kid if it's the last thing we do.'

Mona cried a little at the passion in his voice. They clung together for a while, and finally Mona dried her tears and smiled bravely.

'I'm glad you said that, Butch. I'm real glad you said that. And it will happen, darling. I know that it will.'

Ten o'clock saw Butch thumbing the door bell of the house known as number twenty. The absence of the 'For Sale' notice in the front yard caused him no surprise and the minimum of concern. It did not surprise him that the curtains were on the windows. He was gradually reaching the stage where nothing short of the sky falling would cause him to bat an eyelash.

'My dear Butch! How nice to see you again. And right on time! Do come in, my dear fellow. Do come in.'

In the living-room Alfred Jones offered him a glass of wine. Butch saw the danger in swallowing anything given him by the blue-eyed man and refused.

'Please yourself, of course, Butch. And now, what do you say to us getting straight down to business? The preliminaries have been disposed of and we can take the next step towards perfection. By the way, Butch, you have not suffered any twinge of what you refer to as conscience? No change of mind?'

'I'm right with you, Alfred,' Butch replied gravely.

'Splendid. Splendid. Come with me then.'

Jones led him into the kitchen and opened the door that should have given direct access to the back yard. Of course it merely served as the entrance to the secret chamber where the bank of panels on either side of the large screen twinkled and glinted.

'Take that chair opposite the monitor, Butch.'

The 'monitor' proved to be an oval-shaped panel with half a dozen switches on it and a tiny TV-like screen in the centre. Butch sat down obediently and waited.

'What now?' he asked, striving to keep any tell-tale tremor from his tone.

'Now, my dear boy, we are going to make contact with my other agents. It is essential that each link in the chain is made aware of the existence of the other . . . I'll supply you with the code numbers and the relevant addresses. It is an exercise which I'm certain you are going to enjoy. Afterwards you will be given the first, basic instructions.'

Butch watched with bated breath while he opened a drawer at his side and brought forth a small book bound in black leather. It seemed that good fortune might favour him after all. Jones opened the book at the first page and laid it against the instrument panel.

'Initially, you must dial — Butch! What are you doing? Have you lost control of yourself?'

This was screeched as Butch grabbed the book and jumped up from the chair. He stood off a yard from Jones and whipped a .38 revolver from his pocket, praying that lead bullets would be effective against the alien.

'Don't move, Alfred. Don't move, I tell you!'

With a yell of rage, Jones lunged forward at Butch. Butch's finger squeezed the trigger, once, twice, in rapid succession. He fired without compunction, without any sensation of remorse whatever. He saw Alfred Jones being flung backwards in a whirl of arms and legs.

Jones hit the wall opposite the instrument panels with a thud. He slithered to the floor, gasping, muttering in some strange language that was beyond Butch's ability to comprehend.

In the distance Butch heard a door being hurled open. Heavy feet pounded in the entrance hallway of the house. On the floor, Jones sneered at him, his expression causing the blood to curdle in his veins. His glasses had fallen off and those blue eyes came at the truck driver like laser beams.

'You can't kill me, Butch. I am not mortal as you are. Look at me, Butch. Do it quickly, I tell you! I'm going, but I must take you with me . . . '

'No, no!' Butch screamed. In terror he whirled to the flickering instrument panels, triggering at the large screen, at the winking lights.

'Don't do it, Butch! Don't — '

There was a mighty explosion that rocked the room and sent Butch lurching backwards to strike the kitchen door with his shoulders. The door splintered and he fell through, seeing a tongue of crimson flame lick hungrily towards Jones.

Followed a peal of agony such as Butch had never heard before in his life, and the like of which he never wanted to hear again. Someone was gripping his arm and pulling him towards the house. A voice vibrated over the tremendous crackling and roaring of the fire.

'Did you get the book?' The speaker was the professor, John Davies.

'Book? What book? No, I didn't get it . . . What — '

'You've got it in your hand, Butch. Let me have it. Hustle on out to the street before you're scorched.'

In the street the fire tenders were waiting. So was a large crowd of Butch's neighbours on Willow Road. Three or four of them came towards him, but Frank Hartman clutched his elbow and guided him to one side.

'Keep quiet. Not a word. Say, what the hell has happened to that fire? The house should have caught by now . . . '

The house had not caught fire, as it happened. The amazing thing was that, by then, there was no trace of flame or smoke coming from the rear of the building.

Butch broke away from the detective and raced up the driveway, ignoring the warning yells from police officials. He charged along by the garage until he reached the back yard of number twenty. There, he halted, pulling gulps of night air to his lungs. There was absolutely no trace of a fire. The rear of the house looked as it ought to look in normal circumstances. There was the blank wall of the building, with nothing but the door that gave access to the kitchen visible. The secret chamber had vanished completely.

Two police officers took Butch's arms and propelled him to the front. Another police officer was emerging from the house at that moment. He had his hat off and was scratching his head in perplexity.

'There's no one living there at all, Lieutenant. The joint's as empty as my pocket on the day before pay-day.'

Butch did then what many a stronger man might have done earlier: he fainted.

★   ★   ★

He stirred in his bed to discover that the sun was well up in the sky. He turned his head to glance at the neighbouring bed and smiled faintly when he saw the reassuring tendrils of silky hair protruding from the edge of the cover.

He was tip-toeing towards Mona's bed when the telephone suddenly burred and went on burring insistently.

'Oh, damn,' he growled when Mona sat up and regarded him sleepily. 'Just when I figured how romantic it would be to kiss you awake.'

'Never mind, darling,' Mona laughed. 'Your intentions were good. You'd better hurry and find out who it is. It might be the manager of the holiday chalets, wanting a firm confirmation for the booking you made yesterday . . . '

It was the voice of Frank Hartman which greeted Butch when he had closed the door of the living-room behind him and picked up the receiver. He knew a quick gathering of tension in his chest.

'What is it, Frank?'

'Thought you'd like to hear the latest, Butch. We've just finished the round-up of those people whose addresses were noted in the book. And you know what?'

'What?' Butch rasped, wondering why Hartman was dragging out the suspense. 'You didn't tell me anything about that round-up so far, Frank. You kept putting me off. What happened? What did they say about Jones?'

'Nothing,' the F.B.I. man informed him tersely. He enlarged swiftly. 'They were all dead, Butch. Every man-jack of them. In each case it looked as though they'd had sudden heart attacks. As far as we can judge they all expired on the night of the fire at number twenty. Can you beat it?'

'No, I can't, Frank.' Butch's tone was husky. 'I can't even begin to understand it. Do — do you really think we've heard the last of Alfred Jones, Frank? After all, that planet must be there. Those people must be there . . . '

'The possibility hasn't escaped me, Butch. The only thing we can do is live in hope and be vigilant. You bet we're going to be vigilant from this out. Why, if that story had been allowed to leak to the — '

'But it didn't leak out. The three of us

are the only people who know the truth. It has got to stay that way.'

'Don't worry, Butch. It's going to stay that way. I'd advise you to forget it. I'm not saying that you will, but you've got to try, and so have I. Good hunting, chum.'

'The same to you. Be seeing you, Frank.'

Butch replaced the receiver and stood for a moment, gazing into space. Then he sighed and gave his wide shoulders a shrug. He headed into the kitchen to get the stove burning and make coffee for himself and Mona.

THE END

Other titles in the
Linford Mystery Library:

DEATH CALLED AT NIGHT

R. A. Bennett

Jimmy Ellis believes his parents have died in a car crash when as a young boy he is taken to live with relatives in Australia. The years pass happily, then the nightmare comes. Terrifying images flit through his mind in the dark — all through the eyes of a child, a witness to grisly events seventeen years before. He begins to delve into the past, and soon he finds himself on the trail of a double murderer — a murderer who is prepared to kill again.

THE DEAD TALE-TELLERS

John Newton Chance

Jonathan Blake always kept appointments. He had kept many, in all sorts of places, at all sorts of times, but never one like that one he kept in the house in the woods in the fading light of an October day. It seemed a perfect, peaceful place to visit and perhaps take tea and muffins round the fire. But at this appointment his footsteps dragged, for he knew that inside the house the men with whom he had that date were already dead . . .

THE CALIGARI COMPLEX

Basil Copper

Mike Faraday, the laconic L.A. private investigator, is called in when macabre happenings threaten the Martin-Hannaway Corporation. Fires, accidents and sudden death are involved; one of the partners, James Hannaway, inexplicably fell off a monster crane. Mike is soon entangled in a web of murder, treachery and deceit and through it all a sinister figure flits; something out of a nightmare. Who is hiding beneath the mask of Cesare, the somnambulist? Mike has a tough time finding out.

MIX ME A MURDER

Leo Grex

A drugged girl, a crook with a secret, a doctor with a dubious past, and murder during a shooting affray — described as a 'duel' by the Press — become part of a developing mystery in which a concealed denouement is unravelled only when the last danger threatens. Even then, the drama becomes a race against time and death when Detective Chief Superintendent Gary Bull insists on playing his key role of hostage to danger.

DEAD END IN MAYFAIR

Leonard Gribble

In another Yard case for Commander Anthony Slade, there is blackmail at London's latest night spot. Ruth Graham, a journalist, and Stephen Blaine, a blackmail victim, pit their wits against unusual odds when sudden violence erupts. Then Slade has to direct the 'Met' in a gruelling bout of police work, which involves a drugs gang and a titled mastermind who has developed blackmail into a lucrative practice. The climax to the case is both startling and brutal.